Whispers of Seabreeze Bay

WHISPERS OF SEABREEZE BAY

By Crystal Sky

WHISPERS OF SEABREEZE BAY

CHAPTER ONE: HOMECOMING

The coastal road stretched out before Sarah Montgomery, its curves and bends reminiscent of her life's twists in recent months. She gripped the steering wheel of her old, reliable car as it rolled into the charming town of Seabreeze Bay, her childhood sanctuary. The sun hung low on the horizon, casting a warm, golden glow over the familiar landscape, and as she drove, her thoughts were weighed down by the heavy remnants of a love that had crumbled to dust.

In her rearview mirror, the city lights faded like distant memories. It was a breakup that had sent shockwaves through her heart, leaving fragments of what once was. Sarah's eyes flickered with remnants of tears she'd shed on the long journey back to Seabreeze Bay, but her determination to heal was a beacon guiding her home.

Seabreeze Bay welcomed her with open arms. The air was thick with the salty scent of the sea, carrying promises of healing and renewal. She navigated the winding coastal road with a sense of nostalgia and longing, passing by the familiar landmarks that had witnessed the chapters of her life.

With each mile she left behind, Sarah felt the weight of her past relationship slowly lifting, like the fog that often clung to the early morning coastline. She knew returning to where she had grown up was her best chance at mending a broken heart.

As her car rounded a bend, revealing the first glimpse of Seabreeze Bay's charming town center, Sarah couldn't help but think of the days when she'd been carefree, when the scent of sunscreen and the laughter of friends had filled her summers. Those memories seemed distant, like a photograph that had aged with time.

With a deep breath, Sarah made a silent promise to herself: Seabreeze Bay would be her sanctuary, a place to find solace, rediscover herself, and, just maybe, uncover the possibility of love anew. The town that had witnessed her growth would now bear witness to her healing. And so, with each passing mile, Sarah's journey to mend her heart began in earnest, guided by the whispers of Seabreeze Bay.

As Sarah's car rolled through Seabreeze Bay's quaint streets, she couldn't help but feel that the town held a silent promise of healing.

The tires of her old car hummed a comforting melody, each rotation a step closer to the solace she sought. But suddenly, a shudder rippled through the vehicle, and Sarah's heart sank. The rhythmic hum turned into a dissonant groan. She knew that sound all too well — a flat tire. It seemed as if even the universe was determined to test her resilience.

With a heavy sigh, Sarah maneuvered her car to the side of the road; the shoulder dotted with wildflowers and a view of the ocean waves crashing on the rocks. She felt a familiar frustration bubbling up within her, a mirror to the emotional turmoil that had led her back to this familiar place.

As she stepped out of the car, Sarah's gaze drifted to the horizon, where the sea met the sky, an unending expanse that seemed to hold answers to life's most perplexing questions. But for now, her focus was on the flat tire and the lug nuts that seemed to mock her determination.

Just as Sarah was about to give in to the mounting frustration, a friendly voice broke through the solitude of her tire-changing battle.

"Need a hand?" The voice was warm and inviting, a lifeline in her need.

Startled, Sarah turned to find a man approaching. He was tall and ruggedly handsome, with slightly messy hair and paint-stained hands. His presence was as unexpected as the flat tire itself, but the kindness in his eyes instantly put her at ease.

A hesitant smile tugged at the corners of Sarah's lips as she realized that help had arrived when she needed it most. "Yes, please," she replied, her voice a blend of gratitude and relief.

Under the bright coastal sun, Ethan Brooks worked with practiced ease, his hands swift and sure as he replaced the flat tire. He moved with a grace that came from years of experience, and all the while, he weaved his humorous anecdotes into the conversation.

Sarah couldn't help but laugh as he recounted a tale about a mishap involving paint cans that had left him with those paint-stained hands of his. His sense of humor was like a refreshing breeze on a scorching summer day, and it was impossible not to be captivated.

Amid the laughter and the sound of lug nuts tightening, Sarah felt a lightness in her heart that she hadn't experienced in a long time. It was as if the weight of her recent breakup was slowly lifted, replaced by a sense of connection with this kind stranger.

As the final lug nut securely sealed Sarah's tire, she felt a sense of gratitude. Ethan's unexpected act of kindness had not only saved her from a roadside ordeal but had also lifted her spirits. She looked at him, her eyes shining with laughter from their shared anecdotes.

Ethan wiped his hands on the rag again, his smile as warm as the sun above. "You're all set now," he said, a hint of satisfaction in his voice.

Sarah nodded appreciatively. "Thank you. I really can't thank you enough."

Ethan shrugged with a modesty that only added to his charm. "Just being a good Samaritan," he said with a wink. "By the way, I'm Ethan."

He chuckled, his gaze meeting hers with a hint of curiosity. "Well, if you're not in a hurry, how about joining me for a coffee? There's a charming little café just a short drive from here."

Sarah hesitated, her mind racing with the unfamiliarity of the situation. But then she remembered the undeniable connection she'd felt during their interaction. Ethan's easygoing charm and how he had made her laugh drew her in.

With a tentative smile, she replied, "I suppose I have a little time; my bed and breakfast check-in isn't for a couple of hours. Coffee sounds wonderful."

Ethan's smile widened, and he gestured for her to follow him to his car. As they drove to the nearby café, Sarah couldn't help but feel a sense of anticipation building within her. The chance encounter that had started with a flat tire was now evolving into something more—a budding friendship with the promise of new beginnings.

The café, nestled along a quiet street, exuded a cozy charm. They stepped inside, and as Sarah and Ethan settled into a corner booth, the aroma of freshly brewed coffee enveloped them. Over cups of coffee and shared stories, it was here that the next chapter of their journey would begin with two souls drawn together by fate and a longing for connection in the heartwarming setting of Seabreeze Bay.

And so, amid a chance encounter and shared laughter, the threads of connection between Sarah and Ethan began to weave their own story. Heavy with their burdens, two hearts had found respite in each other's company, and at that moment, hope began to bloom again.

Sarah felt a spark of connection. It was a chance encounter neither of them could have predicted, but sometimes, in the most unexpected places and moments, the heart finds its way back to hope.

The café's quaint charm set the perfect stage for Sarah and Ethan's budding connection. With their hands wrapped around cups of steaming coffee, they delved deeper into their lives, sharing their stories under the soft glow of warm, intimate lighting.

Sarah's eyes, the color of the ocean on a clear day, held a hint of vulnerability as she spoke of her recent heartbreak. "I just needed to come back here," she admitted, her voice tinged with emotion. "This town, these shores... they hold memories of happier times, and I thought maybe being here would help me heal."

Ethan's gaze softened, and he reached across the table to gently cover her hand. "Sometimes, returning to the places where we find solace is the first step to healing," he said, his voice a soothing balm to her wounded heart.

Sarah took a deep breath, the scent of freshly ground coffee beans filling her senses. "And what about you, Ethan? What brings you to Seabreeze Bay?"

A faint smile graced Ethan's lips as he considered her question. "I've lived here for several years," he replied, his eyes sparkling with a hint of mystery. "This town, these shores... they soon became my muse, and I decided to stay. I'm an artist, you see. I paint the beauty of Seabreeze Bay, the stories it holds, and the emotions it awakens."

Intrigued, Sarah leaned forward, her curiosity piqued. "Tell me more," she urged, her heart beginning to flutter with newfound interest.

Ethan hesitated for a moment as if deciding how much to reveal. "Well," he began, his voice taking on a softer tone, "each painting I create holds a piece of my soul. They tell stories of love, loss, and the enduring spirit of this town. But there are some secrets, emotions so raw and personal that I've kept them hidden even in my art."

Sarah nodded, understanding the depths of emotion that could be poured into creative expressions. "It must be amazing to have such a deep connection to a place, to create something beautiful from it."

Ethan's eyes locked onto hers, his gaze intense yet tender. "It is," he agreed, "but sometimes, it takes more than just a beautiful canvas to find inspiration. Sometimes, it takes meeting someone who brings color and light into your world when you least expect it."

Sarah felt her heart skip a beat at his words, the warmth of their connection radiating like the coastal sunsets they both cherished. At that moment, as the café buzzed around them with the hum of life, Sarah couldn't help but wonder if Seabreeze Bay had orchestrated their chance meeting for a reason. Perhaps, in the depths of the town's whispers, her heart had found a new melody that resonated with the promise of love, renewal, and the artistry of two souls discovering each other against the backdrop of a coastal paradise.

CHAPTER TWO: PAINTED SECRETS

Sarah soon settled into a cozy bed-and-breakfast on the outskirts of Seabreeze Bay. The quaint cottage, nestled amidst blooming gardens and surrounded by the soothing sounds of the ocean, provided the perfect refuge for her healing heart. The room's floral decor and the soft sea breeze that rustled the curtains whispered promises of tranquility and renewal.

As the days passed, Sarah found herself increasingly drawn to Ethan. Their coffee date had been a revelation, a glimpse into a man whose artistry seemed as boundless as the horizon. She admired his gentle demeanor and how he had eased her pain with laughter, but the spark of attraction that flickered in their shared moments kept her curious.

One sunny afternoon, as Sarah's heart yearned for a change of scenery, she decided to stroll along the winding coastal paths. Her feet carried her closer to the shoreline, where the rhythmic waves sang their song of healing and hope.

With each step, the scent of salt and sea wrapped around her, enveloping her in a familiar embrace. Sarah felt as though the air was infused with the whispers of Seabreeze Bay. She couldn't shake the feeling that this town held secrets waiting to be unveiled.

As if guided by fate, Sarah meandered farther down the coastline. And then, she stumbled upon it—a hidden art studio tucked away in a cluster of beachside cottages. Its wooden door, held ajar by a rock, painted in vibrant blues and greens, beckoned her closer.

Curiosity got the better of her, and she slipped past the open door, her heart quickening with each creak of the floorboards. Inside, her eyes widened with awe and wonder. The studio was a treasure trove of color and creativity, where dreams were given life on canvas.

Vibrant landscapes and abstract masterpieces adorned the walls, each painting a testament to the talent that resided within these walls. The studio seemed to breathe with the passion of its creator.

Her fingers brushed the edge of a striking seascape, and seeing the signature in the corner, she realized with awe that Ethan was the brilliant artist behind these works. The beauty of Seabreeze Bay, the town's soul, had found its way onto these canvases through his skilled hands.

As she stood amidst the art, Sarah felt a renewed sense of connection, as if the whispers of the bay had guided her here. She knew there was more to discover, more to uncover about the man whose laughter had mended her heart and whose art had now woven its way into her soul.

With a heart filled with newfound curiosity and a sense of intrigue, Sarah quietly left the hidden art studio, her footsteps light as she ventured back into the world beyond. She was now on a journey to heal her own heart and unravel the painted secrets of Seabreeze Bay, one brushstroke at a time.

Sarah's discovery of Ethan's art had ignited a curiosity that refused to be extinguished. As the sun cast its golden glow over Seabreeze Bay each day, her thoughts gravitated toward the enigmatic artist she had met. She was drawn to the hidden art studio like a sailor lured by the siren's song, her heart, and mind equally captivated.

On another sunny morning, her intrigue got the best of her, and she returned to the enchanting studio. The soft chime of a bell welcomed her as she stepped inside.

This time, the sight that greeted her was nothing short of mesmerizing. Ethan stood before an easel, his hands moving with the grace of a conductor as he orchestrated the symphony of colors on the canvas. His eyes were locked onto his work, his expression a fusion of concentration and passion.

The seascape that unfurled under his deft touch was a masterpiece in progress. Waves danced with a vibrant cadence, cliffs stood proud and stubborn, and the sky promised endless horizons. It was Seabreeze Bay's soul, immortalized on canvas.

Sarah couldn't tear her gaze away from his artist's hands, which seemed to possess an innate connection to the hues and emotions that swirled within the paint. She was utterly captivated, the air in the studio humming with creative energy.

Finally, Ethan paused, his eyes meeting Sarah's, and a warm smile graced his lips. "Sarah," he greeted, setting his brush aside, "I didn't expect to see you here."

She stepped closer, her voice a hushed admiration, "I found your cottage, but you weren't there last time; I had to return. Your art... It's incredible. It's like you've captured the heartbeat of this place."

Ethan's cheeks tinged with a faint blush at her words. "Thank you," he replied humbly, a genuine appreciation for her appreciation in his eyes. "Art is my way of connecting with the soul of this town, of capturing the beauty that surrounds us."

Sarah couldn't help but be drawn into the conversation about art, its magic, and its ability to convey the inexpressible. She shared her experiences with creative pursuits, how they had been a sanctuary for her in times of need, a way to translate her emotions into something tangible.

As the words flowed between them, Sarah's heart beat rhythmically with the dialogue. Their connection went beyond casual acquaintance; it was a resonance of souls, two individuals finding a profound kinship through their shared love for art.

Then, fueled by the warmth of their conversation and the nearby easel, Sarah's curiosity led her to make a spontaneous decision. She looked at Ethan with a glint of vulnerability and excitement in her eyes. "Would you... teach me how to paint?" she asked, the words carrying a plea that surpassed mere curiosity.

Ethan's gaze held a mixture of understanding and genuine delight. "I'd be honored," he replied, his voice soft, like the brushstroke of a gentle sky sweeping across a canvas.

With that simple agreement, their worlds began to merge even further. Ethan set up a fresh easel. Sarah's first tentative brushstrokes traced the outlines of Seabreeze Bay, and as Ethan guided her hand, they painted not just colors and lines but the beginning of a shared journey—a journey into the depths of their souls and the uncharted waters of their hearts.

As the hours passed, they created, side by side, a duet of creativity, their bodies and minds in harmonious rhythm. And in the act of painting, their chemistry deepened, the canvas mirroring the connection that had sparked between them. The studio became a sanctuary of shared secrets, whispered aspirations, and unspoken desires.

Sarah couldn't help but feel that the whispers of Seabreeze Bay had guided her here for a reason beyond the solace she sought. In the vibrant strokes of their shared creativity, she found healing and the possibility of a love story painted with the colors of a coastal paradise—a love story that held the promise of intrigue, passion, and an artistic bond that defied the ordinary.

Their shared painting sessions had become a refuge for Sarah and Ethan, a place where colors and emotions merged on canvas. With each stroke, they deepened their connection, their brushes whispering secrets that words could not convey. Yet, there were layers to Ethan's art that remained hidden, like a treasure chest waiting to be unlocked.

One day, as the sun cast dappled patterns on the studio floor, Sarah couldn't help but be drawn to a particular piece Ethan had been working on. It depicted a solitary figure standing at the water's edge, gazing at a distant horizon. The emotions in the painting were palpable—a mixture of longing, hope, and a touch of melancholy.

Sarah approached the painting, her eyes fixed on the enigmatic figure. "This one," she began, her voice soft, "it's so full of emotion. What's the story behind it?"

Ethan paused, his gaze locked on the painting as if he could read its unspoken words. His expression grew contemplative, and for a moment, he seemed lost in his thoughts. Finally, he turned to Sarah, his eyes holding a hint of guardedness. "Some paintings," he replied, his voice carrying a weight of unspoken secrets, "hold stories that are too personal, too raw to share."

Sarah felt a pang of curiosity and intrigue. There was a mystery in his words, a hidden depth to his art that beckoned her to explore further. "But I'd love to hear about them someday," she said, her voice a gentle invitation, "when you're ready."

Ethan offered her a faint smile, gratitude mingling with the guardedness in his eyes. "Someday," he agreed, leaving the door to his past just ajar enough to stir Sarah's intrigue.

As they continued to paint side by side, Sarah couldn't help but wonder about the unspoken stories hidden within the canvases surrounding them. She had embarked on a journey of healing and discovery in Seabreeze Bay, but with each layer of paint they added, it became clear that there were depths to Ethan's soul that she was only beginning to uncover.

Their growing friendship held the promise of unearthing the beauty of art and the complexities of the human heart. Sarah was determined to unravel the mysteries behind those unspoken secrets, to learn about the stories that had shaped Ethan into the man he is today. In doing so, she hoped to create a masterpiece of their own—one that blended the hues of understanding, passion, and the gentle strokes of love, all set against the backdrop of a coastal paradise.

On a day that was a blue and gold symphony, the sun casts its warm embrace over Seabreeze Bay. Sarah's heart fluttered with anticipation as she followed Ethan to a secluded part of the beach. It was a spot hidden among the dunes, where the sand whispered stories of the sea, and seashells held secrets of countless tides.

As they arrived, Sarah's eyes widened in delight. A cozy blanket adorned with a basket of delectable treats and a chilled white wine awaited them. The tranquil murmur of the waves provided a soothing backdrop to this enchanting tableau.

Ethan greeted her with a welcoming smile, his eyes dancing with a hint of mischief. "I thought we could use a little beachside picnic today," he said, spreading his arms wide to encompass the picturesque setting.

Sarah's heart swelled with gratitude as she settled onto the blanket. "This is amazing," she replied, her voice filled with warmth. "You didn't have to do all of this."

Ethan's smile was infectious, and he poured each a glass of wine. "I wanted to," he confessed, his gaze never leaving hers. "I thought it would be a perfect way to spend time together."

They clinked their glasses, and the sound seemed to harmonize with the waves. As they savored the delicious fare, their conversation flowed naturally, like the gentle ebb and flow of the tide.

Sarah's laughter bubbled up as she shared her cherished childhood memories of the beach. "My siblings and I used to build the most extravagant sandcastles," she recounted, her eyes sparkling with nostalgia. "And we'd have these epic seagull-chasing races along the shoreline."

Ethan's memories were painted with vivid colors as he shared his experiences. "I have fond memories of collecting seashells with my grandmother," he said, his voice touched with a softness that only sweet recollections could bring. "And there was this magic about discovering hidden treasures in the tide pools."

Their shared love for the beach created a bridge of understanding, naturally connecting their hearts. With the sun warming their skin and the salt-kissed breeze tousling their hair, they lay back on the blanket, fingers entwined, and gazed up at the endless expanse of the sky.

Sarah turned to look at Ethan, her voice soft with affection. "Thank you for this," she said, her gaze filled with warmth and appreciation.

Ethan's eyes met hers, and he squeezed her hand gently. "You're welcome," he replied, his voice tender. "This is our place, Sarah—where we can create new memories together."

In the embrace of the beach's timeless beauty, they lay there, the world fading away, leaving only the two of them and the promise of a love that had been waiting in the tides of Seabreeze Bay. The beach, with its whispered secrets and timeless allure, bore witness to the blossoming of their romance—a love that would paint their lives with the colors of shared dreams and endless possibilities.

As the days in Seabreeze Bay turned into weeks, Sarah and Ethan's connection deepened, transcending the boundaries of mere friendship. They often stayed up late into the night, their conversations a tapestry of dreams and aspirations woven in the quiet darkness.

On one such night, with the moonlight casting a gentle glow through Sarah's cozy bed-and-breakfast windows, they lay side by side on her bed, talking in hushed tones as if sharing secrets with the stars.

Sarah's voice was vulnerable as she confided in Ethan about her past relationships. "I've learned a lot from my past," she admitted, her fingers tracing patterns on the blanket. "Sometimes, we stay in situations that aren't right for us because we're afraid of change."

Ethan nodded, his gaze focused on the ceiling, his past relationships flashing before his eyes. "I know what you mean," he replied softly. "I've been in relationships where I gave too much of myself, and in the end, I lost sight of who I was."

Their stories intertwined, the confessions flowing like a river of shared experiences. They spoke of their lessons, the healed scars, and the bright hopes within them.

Yet, despite the growing chemistry between them, a palpable tension lingered in the air—a hesitation to act on their feelings, born from the fear of potential risks. They had both felt the magnetic pull between them, the undeniable connection that had been growing stronger with each passing day, but the unspoken question hung heavy in the room: What if they were to cross the line from friendship to something more?

Sarah's heart beat in rhythm with the uncertainty that lingered in the air. She looked at Ethan, her voice filled with longing and trepidation. "Ethan," she began, her words carefully chosen, "what if... what if we're meant to be more than just friends?"

Ethan turned to her, his eyes locked onto hers, his heart laid bare. "Sarah," he replied, his voice carrying the weight of unspoken desires, "I've thought about that too. But I'm scared. Scared of risking what we have, of potentially losing this beautiful connection we've built."

In the quiet of that late-night conversation, their unspoken feelings hung between them like stars in the night sky, their hearts caught in the delicate balance between the comfort of friendship and the tantalizing possibility of love. The chemistry that had sparked between them was undeniable, yet they both understood the fragility of their newfound connection.

As they lay there, bathed in moonlight and the warmth of their shared confidences, they knew that the dawn would bring with it a new chapter in their story—one filled with uncertainty, vulnerability, and the promise of love that could either brighten their lives like the sunrise over Seabreeze Bay or vanish like the stars at dawn's first light.

CHAPTER THREE: ARTISTRY UNVEILED

Ethan had always been a man of solitude, finding solace in the quiet moments of creation within his hidden art studio. His vibrant and expressive paintings expressed the beauty and pain of Seabreeze Bay, capturing the essence of the coastal town that had been his sweet muse. Yet, the thought of sharing his art with the world, of unveiling the stories hidden within each canvas, had always filled him with trepidation.

A white envelope arrived at his doorstep one crisp morning, bearing an invitation that sent ripples through his heart. It was an offer to showcase his art at a local gallery event—a chance to step out of the shadows and into the spotlight, to let the world see the beauty and the secrets he had woven into his work.

Ethan hesitated, the weight of uncertainty settling upon his shoulders like an anchor. The prospect of exposing his deepest emotions, the unspoken life stories, left him feeling vulnerable and exposed. What if they didn't understand his art, or worse, what if they saw too much of him in it?

His inner turmoil echoed through the walls of his studio, his paintings reflecting the storm of emotions swirling within him. He knew he had a decision to make that would test the boundaries of his comfort zone and force him to confront his fears.

That evening, as the sun dipped below the horizon, casting Seabreeze Bay in hues of gold and crimson, Ethan found himself sharing his hesitations with Sarah. They had been painting side by side once more, the colors on their canvases merging like the threads of their growing connection.

"Sarah," he began, his voice tinged with uncertainty, "I received an invitation to showcase my art at a local gallery event."

Sarah looked at him, her eyes filled with genuine enthusiasm for his work. "Ethan, that's amazing!" she exclaimed. "Your art deserves to be seen. It's a part of you, and sharing it with the world is a beautiful way to let people into your heart."

Ethan's gaze met hers, and he couldn't help but feel the warmth of her support. "But what if they don't understand it?" he whispered, his vulnerability bare.

Sarah reached out and gently touched his hand, her voice soft and reassuring. "Art is subjective, Ethan. What matters is that it speaks to someone, that it evokes emotions. Your art has touched my heart, and I know it will touch others too."

Sarah smiled brightly in Ethan's art studio. "I know," she began, "how about I help you prepare for the art show? We can make it a collaboration."

Ethan's eyes lit up at the suggestion. Working with Sarah, blending their unique artistic styles, felt like a dream come true. "I'd love that," he replied, his voice filled with enthusiasm.

As they continued to talk, the weight of Ethan's decision began to lift. With Sarah's encouragement and the promise of her unwavering support, he decided to take a leap of faith. He would accept the invitation to showcase his art, knowing it was a chance to share his talent and a piece of his soul with the world.

Their collaboration began with a blank canvas stretched before them, waiting to be transformed into a masterpiece that would grace the gallery walls. Sarah brought her love for vibrant colors and ethereal landscapes. At the same time, Ethan's talent for capturing the essence of Seabreeze Bay infused each brushstroke with a deep sense of nostalgia and longing.

Their artistic visions melded as they worked together, creating a harmony that transcended mere collaboration. It was as if their souls had found a common language in the colors and shapes they painted—a language that spoke of connection, understanding, and the growing intimacy between them.

Their hands moved in tandem, their bodies swaying to an unspoken rhythm, and the lines between friendship and romance blurred like the colors on their canvas. Once a sanctuary for Ethan's solitary artistry, the studio had transformed into a haven where two hearts beat as one.

Their connection deepened with every brushstroke and every shared moment. Late nights were now filled with laughter and whispered confidences as their bond evolved into something more profound and meaningful than either of them had imagined.

As they prepared for the gallery event in the following weeks, Sarah and Ethan's bond deepened even further. Their connection evolved, becoming a profound partnership built on trust, understanding, and shared dreams. Yet, amidst the excitement of the impending showcase, an unspoken tension lingered in the air—a question that hung between them like a whisper in the sea breeze.

What would this new chapter in their lives mean for their growing friendship? And would the unveiling of Ethan's art also reveal the emotions that had been blossoming in the hidden chambers of their hearts? The answers remained tantalizingly out of reach, waiting to be discovered as their journey continued, guided by the whispers of Seabreeze Bay and the promise of an artistic and romantic destiny yet to be revealed.

With the decision to accept the invitation to showcase his art at the local gallery event, Ethan's days were filled with excitement and a touch of nervous anticipation. As he stepped further into the spotlight, he couldn't help but feel grateful for Sarah's unwavering support.

The gallery event drew nearer, and the anticipation in the air was palpable. Sarah and Ethan had created a masterpiece that would leave a lasting impression on the gallery's visitors and painted a love story waiting to be unveiled.

As the lines of their friendship continued to blur, the lingering question between them grew more urgent. What would the gallery event mean for the unspoken emotions that had taken root in their hearts? And would the canvas of their lives be forever altered by the colors of a love that had blossomed within the whispers of Seabreeze Bay?

One day, while painting, a quiet moment settled between Sarah and Ethan in the heart of Ethan's art studio, where vibrant canvases spoke of hidden stories and emotions. The daylight danced through the windows, casting a soft glow on their collaborative masterpiece, and the air seemed charged with the intimacy of shared creativity.

As they dipped their brushes into paint pots, a hush fell over the studio, inviting vulnerability to take place in the space they had built together. Sarah, her eyes reflecting the colors of her emotions, took a deep breath and began to speak.

"You know, Ethan," she began, her voice a gentle murmur, "my grandmother was a remarkable woman. She had this profound love for art. I remember spending hours with her, watching as she painted beautiful landscapes and told me stories about each stroke of her brush."

Ethan listened intently, his own emotions stirred by Sarah's words. He could see the love and reverence in her eyes as she spoke about her grandmother, and it touched something deep within him.

"Your grandmother sounds incredible," he replied, his voice soft and understanding. "She must have left a lasting impression on you."

Sarah nodded a hint of nostalgia in her smile. "She did. She taught me that art isn't just about colors and shapes;

it's about capturing moments, emotions, and memories on a canvas. It's a way of immortalizing the beauty of life."

Ethan felt a lump in his throat as he thought about the unspoken stories within his art. He knew it was time to share a piece of his past, to unveil the emotions and inspirations that had fueled his work for so long.

"My family has a deep connection to the ocean," he began, conveying reverence. "My great-grandfather was a fisherman, and he used to take me out on his boat when I was a child. Those moments, out on the open sea, watching the sunsets and feeling the power of the ocean, left a profound mark on me."

Sarah looked at Ethan, her eyes filled with curiosity and empathy. She sensed there was more to his story than what he had revealed.

Ethan continued, his voice steady but tinged with vulnerability. "My great-grandfather once told me that the sea held the whispers of generations—stories of love, loss, and the enduring spirit of the sea. It's those whispers that I try to capture in my art."

As their confidences flowed, their vulnerabilities laid bare, Sarah and Ethan forged a deeper emotional connection. The studio, where they had created their masterpiece, had now become a sanctuary for their hearts, where they could share their artistry and innermost selves.

At that moment, surrounded by the colors of their emotions and the echoes of their shared stories, they both felt a profound sense of gratitude for the connection they had found—a connection that went beyond paint and canvas, transcending the boundaries of friendship and hinting at the possibility of a love story that had been waiting in the whispers of Seabreeze Bay.

The night of the gallery event had arrived, casting a blend of excitement and nerves over Sarah and Ethan. The gallery buzzed with anticipation as visitors strolled through the vibrant display of paintings, sculptures, and artistry from the local talents of Seabreeze Bay.

Amidst the collection of artworks, one piece stood out like a beacon—a collaborative masterpiece that bore the unique fusion of Sarah and Ethan's artistic souls. Its colors were a dance of emotions, its strokes whispered secrets, and its presence commanded attention.

As the guests gathered around their creation, Sarah couldn't help but feel a swell of pride for Ethan's talent and their shared accomplishment. The art show was a resounding success, and the admiration in the eyes of the visitors was a testament to the power of their collaboration.

Ethan's eyes met Sarah's, a silent exchange of gratitude and acknowledgment passing between them. In that moment, they shared a deep sense of achievement, knowing that they had created something beautiful together—an artwork that spoke to the hearts of those who gazed upon it.

As the evening unfolded, they celebrated amidst the mingling crowd, basking in the glow of their artistic triumph. The gallery event showcased Ethan's talent and vividly depicted their growing connection. This connection had transcended the boundaries of friendship and was now tinged with the promise of something more.

Amidst the laughter and applause, Sarah and Ethan found themselves drawn to each other, a magnetic pull that defied explanation. They stole a moment alone, hidden in a quiet corner of the gallery, their breaths mingling with the intoxicating scent of paint and passion.

Their eyes locked, and in that tender, stolen moment, their lips met in a gentle kiss that held the promise of love waiting to bloom amidst the colors of their shared dreams.

As they pulled away, their hearts raced with longing, and they knew that this night had changed everything. The art show had unveiled their talents and the depth of their emotions for each other.

In the whispers of Seabreeze Bay, where the tides told tales of love and destiny, Sarah and Ethan had taken their first steps toward a new chapter—a chapter filled with the promise of a love that had blossomed amidst the strokes of their brushes and the colors of their hearts.

With the success of their collaborative masterpiece, their connection had intensified, and the whispers of Seabreeze Bay seemed to sing of romance in the air.

After the art show, their friendship continued to evolve, deepening into something they could no longer deny. The chemistry between them was a magnetic force that drew them closer with each passing moment.

One evening, as the sun dipped below the horizon and painted the sky with hues of orange and pink, Sarah and Ethan found themselves standing on the beach. The gentle lull of the waves and the soft kiss of the sea breeze seemed to mirror the emotions that had been growing between them.

Ethan turned to Sarah, his gaze filled with longing and affection. "Sarah," he began, his voice a whisper in the wind, "I can't ignore what's happening between us anymore."

Sarah met his gaze, her heart pounding with anticipation. "I feel it too, Ethan," she admitted, her voice trembling. "I've never felt a connection like this before."

Their words hung in the air like a promise waiting to be fulfilled. At that moment, as the stars twinkled in the darkening sky, they closed the distance between them. Their lips met in a passionate, heartfelt kiss—a kiss that ignited a fire within their hearts, consuming them with the intensity of their emotions.

Their romance blossomed like spring flowers, each day revealing new layers of their love. Yet, amidst the bliss of their newfound connection, they also grappled with the fear of getting hurt again. Both Sarah and Ethan carried the scars of past relationships, and they knew that love was not without its challenges.

Late nights were now filled with whispered confessions of vulnerability and a shared desire to protect their fragile hearts. They talked about their fears, hesitations, and the possibility of being more wounded by love.

As they lay together on the beach, their fingers intertwined and the waves serenading them, they made a silent promise to each other—a promise to navigate the tides of romance with courage, to embrace the beauty of the present moment, and to cherish the love that had bloomed in the whispers of Seabreeze Bay.

Their journey was far from over, and they knew that challenges lay ahead. But they also knew that love could overcome even the most turbulent tides when nurtured with trust and understanding. In each other's arms, with the sea as their witness, they were ready to embark on this new chapter of their lives—a chapter painted with the colors of love, hope, and the enduring promise of a future together.

CHAPTER FOUR: TIDES OF FRIENDSHIP

Seabreeze Bay's pristine beach stretched out a canvas of golden sands and endless blue waters before Sarah and Ethan. The sun hung high in the sky, casting its warm embrace upon the coastal town, inviting them to spend a day basking in the beauty of the seaside.

With a shared enthusiasm, Sarah and Ethan decided to make the most of this perfect day. They brought their beach towels, a bucket and shovel for sandcastles and an insatiable appetite for adventure. As they stepped onto the sun-warmed sand, laughter and excitement filled the air.

Their first mission was to build the grandest sandcastle Seabreeze Bay had ever seen. With buckets in hand, they scooped up damp sand, shaping it into turrets and towers and molding it into intricate designs. Their hands worked in harmony, like two artists collaborating on a masterpiece.

Sarah couldn't help but laugh as she carefully placed seashells along the walls of their castle. "Ethan, this is the most fun I've had in ages!"

Ethan grinned, the sunlight dancing in his eyes. "I couldn't agree more, Sarah. And you're a natural at this sandcastle-building business!"

Their laughter echoed along the shoreline, blending with the joyful cries of seagulls overhead. As they put the finishing touches on their masterpiece, they marveled at their creation—a sandcastle fit for kings and queens.

With the castle complete, they set off on a leisurely walk along the water's edge, the calm waves lapping at their toes. Their conversation flowed effortlessly, covering deep and light-hearted topics like the tide's ebb and flow.

As they strolled hand in hand, they shared stories of their childhood adventures at the beach, seashell hunts, and the thrill of riding the waves. The shared memories forged a deeper bond, a sense of belonging that transcended the friendship label.

Before long, the sun's warmth called for a sweet treat, and they headed to a nearby ice cream stand. With cones in hand, they sat on a bench overlooking the sea, savoring the creamy indulgence and enjoying the peaceful serenade of the waves.

Their day at the beach was a testament to the genuine camaraderie that had blossomed between them. It was a day of laughter, shared memories, and a deepening friendship that seemed to echo the gentle rhythms of Seabreeze Bay itself.

As the sun descended toward the horizon, casting the sky in shades of pink and gold, Sarah and Ethan knew that their journey together was not defined solely by romance. It was also a journey of friendship—a bond that would stand the test of time, just as the tides of Seabreeze Bay had for generations.

The sun hung low in the sky, casting a warm, golden glow over the beach as Sarah and Ethan sat side by side on their towels. The sound of the gentle waves washing ashore created a soothing backdrop for their conversation—a conversation that was about to delve into the depths of their hearts.

Sarah took a deep breath, her gaze fixed on the horizon as if drawing strength from the sea. She turned toward Ethan, her eyes reflecting vulnerability as she began to speak.

"Ethan," she began, her voice carrying the weight of her past, "there's something I haven't told you about my last relationship."

Ethan turned to her, his eyes filled with concern and understanding. He knew that Sarah had carried the scars of heartbreak, and he was ready to listen, to be the friend she needed.

Sarah hesitated momentarily, then continued, her voice tinged with pain and resolve. "I was with him for five years. We were planning our future together, talking about marriage and a family. But things started to change. He became distant, started working late, and I sensed something was off."

Ethan listened attentively, his heart aching for the pain she had endured. He couldn't help but admire her courage in opening up about her past. He wanted to be there for her, to offer his understanding and support.

"Then one day," Sarah continued, her voice quivering, "I found out he had been seeing someone else. It was like a punch to the gut, Ethan. I confronted him, and he didn't even deny it. He just... walked away."

As she spoke, tears welled in Sarah's eyes, and Ethan reached out to gently squeeze her hand, offering his silent support.

"I felt so broken," she confessed, her voice barely above a whisper. "I questioned everything—my judgment, my worth, everything. It will take me time to heal from that, to trust again."

Ethan leaned in closer, his voice soft and reassuring. "I'm so sorry, Sarah," he said softly, his voice laced with empathy. "No one should have to go through something like that."

Sarah took a deep breath, her eyes meeting Ethan's with gratitude for his understanding. She knew that in him, she had found a friend who listened and truly understood the depth of her emotions.

As they sat together on the beach, the weight of their shared secrets lifted like a burden carried by the sea. Sarah and Ethan had bared their souls to each other, forging a bond that transcended friendship. They were confidants in the truest sense, and in their shared vulnerability, they had discovered a connection that would weather the tides of time, just as Seabreeze Bay had for centuries.

With the sea as their witness, they leaned on each other, finding solace and strength in their shared vulnerability. And as the stars began to twinkle in the darkening sky, they couldn't help but wonder what new secrets the future might hold for them—secrets that would be unveiled in the whispers of Seabreeze Bay.

As the day transitioned into evening, the vibrant hues of the sunset gave way to a star-studded sky over Seabreeze Bay. Sarah and Ethan found themselves at the heart of a beachside bonfire, surrounded by locals who exuded warmth and camaraderie.

The crackling bonfire sent sparks dancing into the night, casting a flickering light that illuminated the faces of those gathered around. Conversations flowed like the gentle tide, and laughter echoed in the sea breeze as the tight-knit community celebrated the beauty of their coastal town.

Ethan and Sarah had been warmly welcomed into the fold, their presence seamlessly woven into the group's fabric. With sand between their toes and the scent of salt in the air, they joined the festivities with open hearts.

A lively game of beach volleyball had begun, and Sarah and Ethan eagerly joined the teams. The competition was spirited, but the joy of being part of this close community mattered most. Sarah's infectious laughter and Ethan's easygoing nature made them a natural fit, earning them cheers and applause from their fellow beachgoers.

After the game, as the bonfire's flames danced higher, the group settled around it, toasting marshmallows on long sticks. The sweet aroma filled the air, blending with the scent of the sea. Sarah couldn't help but smile as she watched the marshmallows turn golden brown, realizing she felt a sense of belonging and connection she hadn't experienced in a long time.

Ethan, too, was impressed by how well Sarah fit into the community. Her ability to connect with people and her genuine enthusiasm for life endeared her to those around her. He felt grateful for the chance to share this moment with her and be part of a community that embraced them both.

As they sat by the bonfire, marshmallow sticks in hand and laughter in their hearts, Sarah and Ethan shared a silent understanding. They had found a place where they were accepted, a community that felt like family, and a friendship growing into something even more meaningful.

Under the starry sky, amidst the laughter and the gentle crackling of the fire, they couldn't help but wonder what new adventures and connections Seabreeze Bay would bring into their lives. The bonfire symbolized the warmth and the bonds they had found in this coastal town, a reminder that sometimes, the most precious moments were those spent with the people who welcomed you with open arms.

The bonfire had dwindled to glowing embers, and most of the beachgoers had bid their farewells, leaving Sarah and Ethan alone on the tranquil shores of Seabreeze Bay. The stars overhead sparkled like a thousand diamonds in the dark velvet sky, casting a dreamy, ethereal glow over the sea.

Sarah and Ethan found a comfortable spot in the sand, their shoulders brushing as they gazed at the vast expanse of stars. Gentle waves lapping at the shore were a soothing backdrop to their conversation.

Sarah spoke first, her voice a soft murmur in the night air. "Ethan, I've always been drawn to the stars. As a child, I used to lie on the grass in my backyard, staring at the night sky and dreaming of far-off places."

Ethan smiled, his eyes reflecting the starlight above. "I can see why. There's something magical about the night sky, isn't there? It's like it holds all our dreams and aspirations, just waiting for us to reach out and grab them."

Sarah glanced at Ethan, her heart warming at his understanding. She had never met anyone who seemed to connect with her so effortlessly. "It's funny," she continued, her voice tinged with introspection, "I thought coming back to Seabreeze Bay was about finding solace, but it's become so much more than that."

Ethan turned to her, his gaze gentle but curious. "More than solace? How so?"

Sarah paused, her eyes tracing the constellations above as if seeking guidance from the stars. "I think I came here to heal, to mend my broken heart. But now I realize that Seabreeze Bay isn't just a place of healing. It's where I've found something I didn't know I was missing."

Ethan's heart skipped a beat at her words. He had felt a connection with Sarah from the moment they met, but hearing her express her feelings heartfeltly touched him deeply. "And what is it that you've found, Sarah?"

Sarah turned her gaze to Ethan, her eyes locking onto his with a mixture of vulnerability and hope. "I've found a friend, Ethan. A true friend who understands me, who listens without judgment, and who makes me feel like I belong."

Ethan's heart swelled with emotion as he looked into Sarah's eyes. He had been drawn to her from the start, and now he knew their connection was exceptional. "I feel the same way, Sarah," he admitted, his voice filled with sincerity. "You've brought a sense of light and warmth into my life that I didn't know was missing."

As they lay side by side on the beach, their fingers entwined, they marveled at the beauty of the starlit night. In the quiet moments between their words, they began to realize that the future held endless possibilities, and Seabreeze Bay had become the backdrop for a love story waiting to unfold in the gentle whispers of the sea.

They knew something extraordinary was blossoming between them in their hearts—a connection beyond friendship, a bond that was strengthened by the shared dreams and the starlit conversations that had brought them closer under the vast, twinkling canvas of the night sky.

As the night deepened, Sarah and Ethan found themselves locked in a wordless exchange of glances that held a universe of unspoken emotions. The stars above seemed to shimmer with anticipation, and the gentle caress of the sea breeze carried a sense of longing.

Sarah's heart raced as she met Ethan's gaze, a million thoughts swirling in her mind. She had come to Seabreeze Bay seeking healing and friendship, but now she was confronted with a powerful attraction that she couldn't ignore. Her fingers tingled with the desire to reach and touch him, to bridge the gap between them.

Ethan's thoughts mirrored Sarah's in that moment, his heart pounding as he gazed into her eyes. He had admired her strength and cherished their friendship, but now he couldn't deny his growing desire, the magnetic pull that drew him closer to her. He questioned whether it was too soon, whether they were ready for something more.

The silence stretched between them, each moment feeling like an eternity. It was as if the universe held its breath, waiting for them to choose. They had both been hurt before, scarred by past relationships, and the fear of getting hurt again loomed large.

Sarah broke the silence, her voice a whisper carried away by the sea breeze. "Ethan, I..."

Ethan's heart skipped a beat as he leaned closer, his voice equally hushed. "Sarah, I..."

Their words hung in the air, unfinished sentences that held the weight of their unspoken feelings. At that moment, they realized that the magnetic pull of attraction was undeniable, a force they could no longer resist.

Ethan's fingers gently brushed against Sarah's, their touch sending a jolt of electricity through them both. Sarah's heart soared, her doubts and fears momentarily forgotten as she leaned in closer, her lips trembling with anticipation.

Ethan met her halfway, their lips brushing in a hesitant, exploratory kiss. It was a spark, a connection, an affirmation of the powerful attraction that had ignited between them. Their kiss deepened, passion and longing entwining like the waves that lapped at the shore.

In the quiet of the night, under the starlit sky, Sarah and Ethan made a silent promise to each other—a promise to embrace the spark that had brought them together, to explore the depths of their attraction, and to see where the tides of romance would lead them in the enchanting world of Seabreeze Bay.

CHAPTER FIVE: MOONLIT STROLL

The moon hung low in the night sky, casting a soft, silvery glow over Seabreeze Bay. Sarah and Ethan, their hearts still racing from their earlier kiss, decided to take a moonlit stroll along the pier. The rhythmic sound of the waves kissing the shore created a romantic ambiance, and the cool sea breeze brushed against their faces like a gentle caress.

Their footsteps echoed softly on the wooden boards of the pier as they walked side by side. The moonlight danced on the water's surface, illuminating a shimmering silver path stretching before them. It was as if the world had slowed down, allowing them to savor each moment.

Sarah couldn't help but steal glances at Ethan, her heart filled with a longing that seemed to grow with each passing step. She wanted to reach out and take his hand, to bridge the small but significant gap between them.

Ethan, too, felt the magnetic pull between them, the desire to be closer to Sarah, to explore the connection that had ignited between them. He wondered if he should take the risk, reach for her hand, and let their fingers entwine.

Their hands brushed against each other, a fleeting touch that sent sparks of electricity through them both. It was a silent invitation, a wordless affirmation of the attraction that had brought them to this moment.

Ethan finally turned toward Sarah, his voice a soft murmur in the moonlit night. "Sarah..."

Sarah met his gaze, her eyes filled with anticipation and vulnerability. "Ethan..."

Their voices trailed off, lost in the romantic serenade of the sea. At that moment, beneath the moon's gentle glow, they let go of their fears and embraced the undeniable connection between them.

Their fingers interlocked, creating a bond that felt like destiny. Hand in hand, they continued their moonlit stroll along the pier, each step bringing them closer to a future filled with promise and the sweet magic of romance in the enchanting world of Seabreeze Bay.

Hand in hand, Sarah and Ethan continued their moonlit stroll along the pier, their footsteps echoing softly in the night. The sea whispered its secrets, encouraging them to share more of themselves.

As they walked, they shared stories of their favorite childhood memories in Seabreeze Bay, moments that had shaped their love for the coastal town.

Sarah spoke first, her voice filled with nostalgia. "Ethan, my favorite memories of Seabreeze Bay are with my grandmother. She used to bring me here when I was a little girl. After sunny days at the beach, she'd take me for ice cream at that little shop near the pier."

Ethan listened intently, his heart warming at the image of a young Sarah and her grandmother. "That sounds wonderful," he replied. "What was your favorite flavor?"

Sarah smiled, lost in the memory. "Mint chocolate chip. It was our secret treat, our way of ending a perfect beach day."

Ethan's memories of Seabreeze Bay began to surface, and he couldn't help but share them. "I have fond memories of this place, too, Sarah. My late father used to bring me here to watch the sunset. He taught me how to appreciate the beauty of the sea, the way the colors painted the sky."

Sarah looked at Ethan with a newfound understanding, sensing the depth of his connection to Seabreeze Bay and the importance of those moments with his father. "That sounds like a special bond you had with him."

Ethan nodded, his gaze focused on the moonlit waves. "It was. Those sunsets were like a gift he gave me, a reminder of the beauty surrounding us, even in the darkest moments."

Their shared memories became a bridge, connecting their pasts to their present. As they continued to stroll along the pier, their stories flowed like the sea, creating a deeper understanding of each other's lives and experiences.

In the moonlit night, beneath the watchful gaze of the stars, Sarah and Ethan realized that Seabreeze Bay was more than just a backdrop for their romance. It was where their hearts had found a home, where shared memories and dreams had woven a tapestry of love that would forever bind them together in the enchanting world of Seabreeze Bay.

The pier stretched before them, its wooden boards leading to the edge where the moonlight painted a silver path on the water's surface. Sarah and Ethan had been sharing stories of their past, their hands still entwined, their connection growing with each step.

As they reached the end of the pier, the magnetic pull between them became too powerful to resist. The soft caress of the sea breeze, the rhythmic sound of the waves, and the moonlight conspiring with the universe created exquisite tension.

Sarah turned to face Ethan, her heart pounding with anticipation and longing. Her eyes met his, and in that silent exchange, they both knew that the time had come to let go of their fears and embrace the undeniable attraction that had blossomed between them.

Ethan, his gaze filled with desire and tenderness, leaned in closer. Sarah closed her eyes, her breath catching as their lips met in a sweet and tender kiss. It was a kiss that spoke of shared dreams, shared memories, and a shared affection that had been growing between them.

Their lips moved in perfect harmony, their kiss a testament to the depth of their connection. It felt like the universe had aligned to bring them together at that moment, and the world around them faded insignificantly.

It was a kiss they had both been waiting for, a kiss that felt like the beginning of something beautiful. As they pulled away, their eyes met once more, their expressions a mix of awe and wonder at the profound connection they had discovered in the enchanting world of Seabreeze Bay.

In the moonlit night, with the sea as their witness, Sarah and Ethan knew that their journey was beginning and that the tides of romance had carried them into uncharted waters. But they were ready to explore this new chapter of their lives together, hand in hand, under the gentle guidance of the stars and the whispers of Seabreeze Bay.

After their sweet and tender kiss on the pier's edge, Sarah and Ethan found themselves lost in each other's gaze, the moonlight reflecting in their eyes like twin beacons of hope.

With their fingers still entwined, they shared a moment of quiet reflection, their hearts and minds in perfect synchrony. The sea whispered its secrets, urging them to make promises that would bind their hearts together.

Sarah broke the silence, her voice soft and filled with sincerity. "Ethan, I want you to know that no matter where life takes us, I promise to support and cherish you. I promise to be there for you through the ups and downs, the uncertainties, and the joys."

Ethan smiled, his heart overflowing with emotion. "Sarah, I feel the same way. Life is full of twists and turns, but I promise to navigate it with you, to be your anchor when you need it, and your partner in all life's adventures."

They spoke their promises under the moon, their declarations of love carried away by the sea breeze. It was a moment of vulnerability and truth as they vowed to face the uncertain future together.

The moonlight bathed them in its soft glow, and their whispered promises hung like a beautiful melody. At that moment, Sarah and Ethan knew that they had found something rare and precious in each other—a love that was worth taking risks for, a love that would shine even brighter in the enchanting world of Seabreeze Bay.

The night they had shared was nothing short of magical, a tapestry of shared memories, promises, and a tender kiss beneath the moonlit sky. As the hours passed, the moon descended toward the horizon, making way for the first light of dawn.

Sarah and Ethan, hand in hand, knew it was time to return to their respective homes. The sea had whispered its secrets, and the stars had witnessed the beginning of their romance.

With each step they took, the world around them began to wake, the colors of the sky transitioning from inky black to shades of soft lavender and rosy pink. The first light of daybreak painted the horizon, marking the beginning of a new chapter in their lives.

Sarah's heart was full of hope and love as she looked at Ethan, her eyes reflecting the dawn's early light. "Ethan, this has been the most amazing night of my life."

Ethan smiled, his fingers gently caressing hers. "Mine too, Sarah. I can't wait to see where this journey takes us."

They shared a lingering gaze, their hearts filled with the promise of a future filled with love and adventure. Seabreeze Bay had become the backdrop for their unfolding romance with its healing embrace and the promise of love.

As they reached the point where their paths diverged, they shared one last, sweet kiss, a silent affirmation of their love and the bond they had forged under the moon and stars.

With the first light of dawn as their witness, Sarah and Ethan parted ways, each carrying the memory of that magical night in their hearts. It was the beginning of something beautiful, a love story that had found its place in the enchanting world of Seabreeze Bay.

CHAPTER SIX: SPARKS IGNITE

The sun's afternoon rays gently filtered through Sarah's bedroom window, bathing her in a warm, golden glow. She awoke with a smile, her thoughts drifting to the magical night she had shared with Ethan. The moonlit stroll, their shared memories, and the promises beneath the moon felt like a beautiful dream.

With contentment and anticipation, Sarah rose from her bed, her heart feeling lighter than it had in a long time. She knew that the enchantment of Seabreeze Bay had woven its magic around her, and she couldn't wait to see what the day held.

After a quick shower and a glance in the mirror, Sarah decided to head to the local café, a place she had always loved for its cozy atmosphere and the comforting aroma of freshly brewed coffee. It was a perfect spot to gather her thoughts and savor the memories of the night before.

As Sarah entered the café, the friendly barista greeted her with a warm smile. She ordered her usual coffee, a simple pleasure that never failed to start her day off right.

Just as she reached into her bag for her wallet, a mischievous voice behind her said, "I'll get that for you."

Startled, Sarah turned to find Ethan standing there with a playful grin. He held out his hand, offering to pay for her drink.

"Ethan!" Sarah exclaimed, a delightful surprise washing over her. "You don't have to do that."

Ethan chuckled, his eyes dancing with glee. "Consider it a gift. After all, we did have a pretty amazing night. I was hoping to catch up with you here."

Sarah couldn't help but laugh, her heart fluttering at his gesture. "Well, in that case, thank you." She accepted his offer with a grateful smile, allowing him to pay for her coffee.

As they waited for their drinks, they exchanged knowing glances, the magic of the night before still lingering between them. It was a day filled with promise, a reminder that the enchantment of Seabreeze Bay was far from over.

With their coffees in hand, Sarah and Ethan found a cozy corner in the café where they could continue to savor the moments they had shared and the budding romance that had taken root in the enchanting world of Seabreeze Bay.

As Sarah and Ethan sat in the cozy corner of the café, sipping coffee, a friendly banter began to unfold between them. Their laughter filled the air, and it was as if the enchantment of Seabreeze Bay had cast a spell of playfulness over them.

Ethan set his coffee cup down and leaned in with a mischievous glint in his eye. "Sarah, I can't help but think that our night under the stars was pretty magical. But I feel you might not be as skilled in other areas."

Sarah raised an eyebrow, a playful challenge in her gaze. "Oh? And what area are you suggesting, Ethan?"

Ethan grinned, his playful tone revealing his intentions. "Mini-golf, Sarah. I challenge you to a mini-golf tournament later today."

Sarah couldn't help but laugh at his suggestion. "You're on, Ethan. But be warned—I'm quite the mini-golf champion."

Ethan chuckled; his competitive spirit was evident. "We'll see about that. Loser buys ice cream."

Their playful banter continued, their voices filled with light-hearted teasing and anticipation for the friendly competition ahead. It was a spontaneous decision but added an exciting element to their relationship.

As they finished their coffees, they made plans for the mini-golf tournament, agreeing to meet later at the seaside mini-golf course. It was a challenge that would bring them even closer, a chance to create more memories in the enchanting world of Seabreeze Bay.

With a twinkle in their eyes and the prospect of a fun time ahead, Sarah and Ethan left the café, ready to embrace the playful spirit of their budding romance, and the adventure awaited them on the mini-golf course.

The sun hung in the sky as Sarah and Ethan arrived at the seaside mini-golf course, ready for a light-hearted afternoon of fun and friendly competition. The coastal breeze carried the scent of the sea, and the sound of seagulls overhead added to the cheerful atmosphere.

With putters and colorful golf balls, they embarked on their mini-golf adventure. The course was a whimsical maze of obstacles filled with twists, turns, and challenging holes. Laughter and camaraderie filled the air as they engaged in playful teasing throughout the game.

Sarah couldn't help but admire Ethan's impressive golf skills, while Ethan was equally impressed by Sarah's determination and precision. Each hole brought challenges, and they cheered each other on as they navigated the course.

As they reached the final hole, the competition had reached a fevered pitch. The score was tied, and the winner of this hole would claim victory. The last spot was tricky, with a narrow passage leading to the final cup.

Sarah took her shot first, her ball gliding smoothly through the obstacles and landing tantalizingly close to the cup. Ethan studied the course, his brow furrowed in concentration. With a steady hand, he took his shot, the ball rolling toward the cup.

The suspense was palpable as they watched Ethan's ball. It bumped against the edge of the cup, teetering on the brink of victory before finally dropping in with a satisfying clink.

Ethan turned to Sarah with a triumphant grin. "Looks like I win, Sarah."

Sarah laughed, good-naturedly conceding defeat. "Congratulations, Ethan. You earned it."

But as they stood on the final hole, the anticipation and excitement in the air were electric. With the mini-golf game behind them, they couldn't deny the attraction that had grown between them.

Ethan took a step closer to Sarah, his gaze locked onto hers. "Well, they say that winners get to claim a prize."

Sarah smiled, her heart racing. "And what's the prize, Ethan?"

Without hesitation, Ethan leaned in, capturing Sarah's lips in a sweet and lingering kiss. It was a kiss that sealed their afternoon of mini-golf fun, a kiss filled with the promise of more adventures to come in the enchanting world of Seabreeze Bay.

After their playful and competitive game of mini-golf, Sarah and Ethan decided to stroll along the beach. The sun descended toward the horizon, casting a warm, golden hue over the coastline.

As they walked hand in hand, they eventually found a secluded spot on the beach where they could sit and enjoy the tranquil beauty of the setting sun. The soft sand cradled them as they settled in, the sound of the waves providing a soothing backdrop.

Sarah gazed out at the horizon, her heart feeling full as she watched the sun dip lower and lower, painting the sky with hues of orange and pink. She felt a warmth beside her and turned to find Ethan, his eyes fixed on her with an intensity that sent shivers down her spine.

Ethan reached out, gently tucking a loose strand of hair behind Sarah's ear. His touch was electric, igniting a fire of desire between them. Without a word, he leaned in, capturing her lips in a more passionate kiss than they had ever shared.

Their chemistry was undeniable, their kiss a testament to the deepening connection they felt for each other. It was a stolen moment on the beach, where time seemed to stand still, and the world around them faded into insignificance.

As they finally pulled away, breathless and filled with desire, Sarah and Ethan knew their romance had evolved more profoundly. The enchanting world of Seabreeze Bay had woven its magic around them, and they were ready to embrace the love that had blossomed between them, no matter where the tides of destiny would lead.

As the sun continued its descent, painting the sky with fiery hues, Sarah and Ethan sat together on the beach, their hands still entwined, their hearts laid bare.

Ethan turned to Sarah, his eyes filled with a mixture of emotions. "Sarah, I can't help but feel that our connection has grown stronger and more complex. These past few days with you have been incredible."

Sarah nodded, her own heart echoing his sentiments. "I feel the same way, Ethan. There's something about Seabreeze Bay, about us, unlike anything I've ever experienced."

They shared a moment of silence, the waves crashing gently against the shore as they contemplated the depth of their feelings. Sarah knew that her heart had found a home in Seabreeze Bay, and it was with Ethan.

Ethan continued, his voice filled with a mix of excitement and uncertainty. "I can't deny how much I care about you, Sarah. But it also scares me a little. Love is a beautiful thing, but it can also be unpredictable."

Sarah placed a hand on his cheek, her touch reassuring. "I understand, Ethan. Love can be both wonderful and daunting. But I believe we're meant to explore this new chapter of our relationship together, to see where it takes us."

Their eyes locked, and in that moment, they made a silent promise to navigate the complexities of their feelings and the uncertainties of the future as a team.

As the sun dipped below the horizon, casting the beach in a tranquil twilight, Sarah and Ethan knew their love story was beginning. With the enchanting world of Seabreeze Bay as their witness, they were ready to embrace the beauty and complexity of their emotions, come what may.

CHAPTER SEVEN: A DATE BY THE BAY

The days in Seabreeze Bay were filled with laughter, shared moments, and the deepening of Sarah and Ethan's connection. As the sun dipped below the horizon, casting a warm glow over the coastal town, they sat in Sarah's cozy living room, surrounded by the soft flicker of candlelight.

Ethan turned to Sarah, a sparkle of excitement in his eyes. "You know, Sarah, I've been thinking. We should plan a special date that reflects our unique connection and the beauty of Seabreeze Bay."

Sarah smiled, her heart dancing at the prospect of a romantic evening with Ethan. "I couldn't agree more. But what should it be? Seabreeze Bay has so much to offer."

They both leaned in, their heads almost touching as they began brainstorming ideas for their perfect date. Sarah's voice was filled with anticipation as she spoke. "How about the seafood restaurant by the beach?"

Ethan's eyes lit up with enthusiasm. "That sounds amazing. We could watch the sun dip below the horizon and listen to the waves while we enjoy a delicious meal together."

Sarah nodded in agreement. "And we can bring a blanket to sit on the sand and stargaze after sunset."

Ethan couldn't help but be drawn into Sarah's excitement. "That's a great idea. It's the perfect setting for romance."

As they continued to plan their date, their voices filled the room with ideas and possibilities. They talked about the menu, the music, and the little details that would make the evening unforgettable.

But amidst their planning, there was something more profound at play—a growing connection and an unspoken understanding of the significance of this date. It was a moment for them to celebrate what they had found in each other, savor Seabreeze Bay's beauty, and let their feelings for one another bloom in the soft light of the setting sun.

Sarah and Ethan couldn't wait for the day of their beach date, knowing that it would be a reflection of their unique connection and the enchantment of Seabreeze Bay— a place where love had found its home and where their hearts were free to explore the depths of their feelings for each other.

The day of their special date arrived, and Seabreeze Bay had never looked more enchanting. Sarah and Ethan arrived at the picturesque seaside restaurant overlooking the bay's tranquil waters. It was the perfect setting for a romantic evening.

As the sun began its descent, casting hues of orange and pink across the sky, Sarah and Ethan sat at a candlelit table by the window. The soft glow of the candles illuminated their faces, and the sound of the waves added to the ambiance.

Sarah couldn't help but smile as she looked at Ethan. "This place is incredible, Ethan. Thank you for inviting me."

Ethan returned her smile, his eyes filled with warmth. "It's my pleasure, Sarah. I wanted our date to be as special as our connection."

The evening unfolded in a symphony of delicious seafood, heartfelt conversations, and stolen glances. They talked about their dreams and aspirations, discovering they loved adventure and exploration.

Sarah shared her desire to travel the world, experience new cultures, and capture the beauty of different landscapes through her photography. On the other hand, Ethan spoke passionately about his love for the sea and his dream of sailing to distant shores, capturing the essence of the ocean in his art.

Their dreams and aspirations seemed to align, and their connection deepened with each word they exchanged. The evening was filled with laughter and moments of quiet reflection, the restaurant's stunning view of the bay serving as a backdrop to their burgeoning romance.

As the night wore on and the stars twinkled in the clear sky, Sarah and Ethan knew that this date was a turning point in their relationship. It was a moment to celebrate their connection, shared dreams, and the love blossoming between them.

Under the soft glow of the moon and the stars, Sarah and Ethan continued to explore the depths of their feelings, knowing that Seabreeze Bay had woven its magic around them and their love story was beginning.

After a delightful seaside dinner, Sarah and Ethan extended their romantic evening with a moonlit walk on the beach. The soft, silver glow of the moon cast a romantic aura over Seabreeze Bay, and the sound of the waves beckoned them to the shore.

Hand in hand, they strolled along the sandy beach, the gentle rhythm of their footsteps echoing the beating of their hearts. The stars above shone brighter as if the universe was celebrating their love.

They found a secluded spot, away from the soft glow of the town's lights, where the beach stretched before them. Sarah spread a blanket on the sand, and they lay down, their fingers intertwined and their eyes fixed on the canopy of stars above.

The night sky was an endless tapestry of sparkling jewels, and a sense of awe washed over them as they lay there. Sarah whispered, "It's incredible how vast the universe is, isn't it?"

Ethan nodded, his voice barely above a whisper. "It is. It makes you realize how small we are in the grand scheme."

Sarah turned her gaze toward Ethan, her heart filled with gratitude for this moment. "But in this vast universe, we found each other in Seabreeze Bay."

Ethan's eyes met hers, his expression soft and filled with affection. "Yes, we did, Sarah. And that's something extraordinary."

They lay there, gazing at the stars, appreciating the beauty of the universe and the wonder of finding love in such a special place. It was a quiet moment of connection and reflection, a reminder of the magic that had brought them together in Seabreeze Bay.

As the waves whispered their secrets and the stars continued their silent dance, Sarah and Ethan knew their love story was written in the stars. The enchantment of this coastal town had woven its spell around them, and they were ready to embrace the future, hand in hand, under the watchful gaze of the universe.

As they lay on the blanket, bathed in the moon's soft glow and the shimmering stars, Sarah and Ethan's feelings for each other became undeniable. The magic of the night seemed to amplify their connection, making it impossible to ignore the depth of their emotions.

Ethan turned to Sarah, his eyes filled with tenderness. "Sarah, there's something I need to tell you."

Sarah met his gaze, her heart racing in anticipation of his words. "What is it, Ethan?"

He took a deep breath, his voice barely above a whisper in the quiet of the night. "I love you, Sarah. I've fallen in love with you."

Sarah's heart swelled with emotion, and tears welled up in her eyes. She had felt the same way but was hesitant to speak the words. With a trembling voice, she replied, "Ethan, I love you too, more than I can express."

Their whispered confessions of love hung in the air, a testament to the deep and profound connection they had found in each other. At that moment, there were no doubts, no fears—only the overwhelming certainty that their hearts were meant to be together.

Ethan brushed a tear from Sarah's cheek, his touch gentle and filled with love. "I want to cherish every moment we have together, Sarah. Life is unpredictable, but loving you is worth every moment."

Sarah nodded, her heart full of gratitude for this incredible man beside her. "I love you, Ethan.

Ethan's heart soared at the sound of those three simple words. He had longed to hear them from her, and now that they were spoken, it felt like the sweetest melody.

In that tender moment, their love was no longer a secret or a whispered confession under the stars. It was a truth they both held dear, a bond that had deepened with each passing day in the enchanting world of Seabreeze Bay.

They sealed their promises with a tender kiss under the starlit sky, their connection deepening with each passing second. As the night continued to embrace them, Sarah and Ethan knew that their love was a precious gift they would cherish and nurture in the enchanting world of Seabreeze Bay.

Under the starry sky, with the sound of the waves as their lullaby, Sarah and Ethan shared a moment of quiet reflection after confessing their love for each other. They knew it was a pivotal point in their relationship, a moment they would always treasure.

In those tender moments, their love was no longer a secret or a whispered confession under the stars. It was a truth they both held dear, a bond that had deepened with each passing day in the enchanting world of Seabreeze Bay.

As they parted ways and returned to their homes, the promise of their love hung in the air, a source of strength and inspiration for the challenges and joys ahead. Sarah and

Ethan knew that their romance was a journey worth taking, and with love as their guiding star, they were ready to embrace whatever the future held for them in Seabreeze Bay.

CHAPTER EIGHT: LIGHTHOUSE DISCOVERIES

Seabreeze Bay was bathed in the soft morning light as Sarah and Ethan embarked on a day of exploration. The picturesque lighthouse, perched atop a cliff, was their destination—a symbol of their growing love and the light that had guided them together.

As they approached the lighthouse, its white walls gleaming in the sun, they couldn't help but feel a sense of wonder. The day was filled with promise, and they were ready to create more cherished memories together.

Hand in hand, they climbed the spiral staircase that led to the top of the lighthouse. Their laughter echoed in the narrow passageway with each step, a melody of shared joy.

Finally, they reached the top, and their breath was stolen by the breathtaking views that greeted them. The coastline stretched before them, the sea meeting the sky in an endless horizon. With its azure waters and golden sands, Seabreeze Bay looked like a painting brought to life.

Sarah and Ethan leaned against the railing, their hearts swelling with gratitude for this moment. They watched as seagulls danced on the wind and sailboats glided gracefully over the waves.

But it was more than the scenery that took their breath away—the love and connection they shared. At that moment, they were free, their worries and doubts washed away by the beauty of Seabreeze Bay and the magic of their love.

They were filled with wonder as Sarah and Ethan basked in the breathtaking views from the top of the lighthouse. The beauty of Seabreeze Bay unfolded before them like a treasure waiting to be discovered.

While taking in the scenery, Ethan noticed something unusual—a small, weathered door tucked away in a corner of the lighthouse's observation deck. His curiosity piqued, he nudged Sarah, and they approached the hidden entrance together.

With a gentle push, the door creaked open, revealing a small, secret room bathed in soft, filtered sunlight. The room was adorned with shelves filled with old journals, their pages yellowed with time and filled with handwritten entries.

Sarah and Ethan exchanged surprised glances. It seemed they had stumbled upon a hidden treasure of a different kind—a place where lovers had left heartfelt notes to each other over the years. These journals were a testament to the enduring love stories that had unfolded in Seabreeze Bay.

They began to peruse the pages with reverence, each entry a glimpse into a different chapter of love. The stories were both joyous and heart-wrenching, filled with declarations of love, promises, and memories shared by couples who had stood where they were now.

Sarah's heart swelled with emotion as she read the poignant words of lovers who had come before them. The lighthouse had silently witnessed countless love stories, each as unique and precious as the last.

Inspired by the legacy of love contained in those journals, Ethan turned to Sarah with a twinkle in his eye. "We should leave our love note," he suggested.

Sarah's eyes lit up with delight. Together, they picked up a dusty, forgotten journal and found a blank page. With a shared smile, they began to pen their love note, expressing their feelings for each other in heartfelt words.

Their love note spoke of the adventures they had shared, the laughter that filled their days, and the way their hearts had found a home in each other. It was a promise of love and devotion, a testament to the unique love story they were creating in the enchanting world of Seabreeze Bay.

As they carefully placed the journal back on the shelf, their love note hidden among the others, they felt a deep connection to the lovers who had come before them. They knew their love was now a part of the lighthouse's storied history, and they couldn't wait to see where their journey would take them in the days and years.

As Sarah and Ethan descended from the lighthouse, their hearts still warmed by discovering the hidden love journals; they found themselves on a winding path leading to a secluded spot overlooking the sea. The sun bathed the world in golden hues, and the rhythmic sound of waves added a soothing backdrop to their footsteps.

The moment was serene, a haven of tranquility where their love could blossom without the world's distractions. They settled on a weathered bench, the sea breeze tousling their hair as they gazed out at the endless expanse of ocean.

With the sea stretching out before them, Sarah and Ethan shared stories of their growing love for each other. They spoke of the moments that had drawn them closer—the laughter, the late-night conversations, the stolen glances filled with unspoken desire. It was a narrative of love written in the language of their hearts.

As Sarah spoke of how she felt floating on a sea of happiness whenever she was with Ethan, he couldn't help but smile. He confessed that every moment they spent together was a treasure he cherished, and his heart had found its anchor in her.

A sudden, beautiful spontaneity took hold of Ethan during their tender exchange. Unable to resist the magnetic pull of their emotions, he leaned in, capturing Sarah's lips in a sweet, unexpected kiss.

Time seemed to stand still as their lips met, the world around them fading into insignificance. Sarah's heart raced excitedly, and Ethan's kiss tasted like a promise of their love blossoming.

When they finally parted, their eyes locked in a shared moment of pure connection, they knew that their love was like the sea—vast, deep, and full of mysteries yet to be explored. The surprise kiss deepened their bond, and as they looked at the endless horizon, they couldn't help but feel that their love story was beginning, with Seabreeze Bay as its enchanting backdrop.

That evening, as the sun dipped below the horizon, casting Seabreeze Bay in a tapestry of oranges and pinks, Sarah and Ethan prepared for a magical evening. They had heard about a local beachside dance event, a charming tradition in Seabreeze Bay that drew both locals and visitors alike.

With a sense of anticipation, they made their way to the event. Strings of soft, twinkling lights illuminated the sandy dance floor by the shore, creating an enchanting atmosphere under the starry sky.

The rhythmic melodies of a live band filled the air, and couples swayed gracefully to the music, their silhouettes dancing against the backdrop of the moonlit sea. It was a night when love was celebrated through the language of dance.

Sarah and Ethan joined the crowd, the music pulling them closer together like a magnet. As they took each other's hands, they began to move in time with the music, their bodies swaying in perfect harmony. The world around them faded into the background, and for a while, it was just the two of them and the music of their hearts.

Sarah and Ethan danced under the starry sky and the gentle caress of the sea breeze as if they were the only people in the world. Each step was a testament to their growing connection, a symbol of the love story they were creating in the heart of Seabreeze Bay.

As they twirled and swayed, their eyes locked in a shared moment of pure affection. They could feel the depth of their emotions in how they moved, the music serving as a soundtrack to their blossoming romance.

It was a night filled with stolen glances and whispered words of love. The dance was not just a celebration of their love; it was a declaration of their commitment to each other, a promise to continue writing their love story in the most beautiful ways.

As the night waned and the music played on, Sarah and Ethan knew their love was like a fluid, graceful, and timeless dance. In the heart of Seabreeze Bay, their love story unfolded with every step, and they couldn't wait to see where the music of their hearts would lead them next.

As the beachside dance event drew to a close, Sarah and Ethan found themselves on the tranquil shores of Seabreeze Bay once more. They sat side by side, the grains of sand beneath them, the stars above them, and the sound of the waves as their soothing lullaby.

In this quiet moment, they spoke about their future together, their dreams and aspirations, and the adventures they wished to embark on. With its eternal ebb and flow, the sea seemed to echo their sentiments of everlasting love.

But amid their dreams, they also spoke of a future where their paths would intertwine. They imagined a life in Seabreeze Bay, where every sunrise and sunset would be a celebration of their love.

With the sound of the waves as their witness, they made promises to each other—promises of unwavering support, being each other's rock in times of storm and celebrating every moment of joy that life would bring.

Their hearts were filled with hope and love, and they knew Seabreeze Bay had brought them together for a reason. The magic of this coastal town had not only healed their wounds but had also woven the threads of their love story, creating a tapestry of love and happiness.

As they sat on that moonlit beach, their hands entwined, they promised to cherish each other and the love they had found. The future was uncertain, but they were determined to face it together, with Seabreeze Bay as the backdrop to their ever-evolving love story.

CHAPTER NINE: DOUBTS AND DECISIONS

Seabreeze Bay was bathed in the soft glow of a late afternoon sun as Sarah sat on her favorite bench overlooking the bay. The picturesque scene stretched before her, with the tranquil sea and the azure sky blending into one seamless horizon. But today, Sarah couldn't find solace in the natural beauty that surrounded her.

Like the restless waves gently kissing the shore, her mind was in turmoil. Doubts had crept in over the past few days like unwelcome visitors, and she could no longer ignore them. The weight of her thoughts tugged at her heart, casting a shadow over the love she had discovered with Ethan.

She gazed out at the sea, its vastness reflecting her uncertainty. Sarah had fallen in love, and she had no doubt. The connection she shared with Ethan was unlike anything she had ever experienced, and it had brought her a profound sense of joy and contentment. Yet, there were secrets, secrets that Ethan guarded with a determination that both intrigued and concerned her.

As the gentle breeze ruffled her hair, Sarah questioned her feelings. She knew that love sometimes required trust in the face of uncertainty, but she couldn't help but wonder if she was being naive. Her heart ached for transparency and a deeper understanding of the man she had allowed into her life and spirit.

She sighed, her gaze never leaving the sea. "What are you hiding, Ethan?" she whispered, more to herself than to the vast expanse of water before her.

The whispers of doubt continued to haunt her like the distant echoes of waves crashing against the rocks. Sarah knew she needed to confront her feelings and have an honest conversation with Ethan, but the fear of what she might discover weighed heavily on her heart.

As the sun dipped lower in the sky, Sarah knew the time for decisions was approaching. She couldn't let her doubts fester; she needed to find a way to bridge the gap between them. Seabreeze Bay had been a place of healing and love, and she was determined to ensure it remained so, even if it meant facing uncomfortable truths.

One evening, the sun had dipped below the horizon, casting a warm, golden hue across Seabreeze Bay. Sarah and Ethan decided to walk along the beach, the salty breeze carrying a sense of unease as they strolled in silence, their footsteps in rhythm with the crashing waves.

The tranquility of the beach, which had once been a sanctuary for their burgeoning love, now seemed to mirror the churning uncertainty within Sarah's heart. She couldn't ignore the nagging feeling that there were parts of Ethan he was keeping hidden from her, and it weighed on her like a heavy anchor.

As they walked, Sarah's eyes were fixed on Ethan, her gaze searching for answers she feared she might not find.

She couldn't bear the thought of being in a relationship where secrets were kept, where trust wavered in the shadows.

Finally, she couldn't keep her thoughts to herself any longer. "Ethan," she began, her voice tinged with concern and vulnerability, "I can't help but feel like there are parts of you that you're hiding from me."

Ethan's gaze remained fixed on the distant horizon, his expression troubled. He sighed heavily, his shoulders slumping slightly. "Sarah," he started, his voice gentle yet burdened, "there are things in my past, painful memories and experiences that I haven't shared with you. It's not because I don't trust you or want to keep secrets. It's because I'm afraid of how you'll see me once you know."

Sarah stopped walking, her heart heavy with the weight of his words. She turned to him, her eyes filled with concern and a desire to understand. "Ethan, you don't have to carry your burdens alone. We're in this together, and I want to know all of you."

Ethan finally met her gaze, his eyes reflecting gratitude and hesitation. "Sarah, I promise," he said, his voice soft and filled with sincerity, "when the time is right, I'll tell you everything. I need a little more time to find the courage."

Their footsteps again fell into sync as they resumed walking along the moonlit beach. Sarah knew that trust and love were built on the foundation of understanding and acceptance. Though uncertainty still lingered in the air, she held onto the hope that, in time, their love would overcome the shadows of the past, and their bond would be even more vital for it. Seabreeze Bay, with all its mysteries, would bear witness to their journey, no matter where it led.

In the days following their beachside walk, Sarah was more inexplicably drawn to Ethan's art studio than ever. Each visit was a chance to get closer to the enigmatic artist she had fallen in love with, and yet, it also fueled her curiosity about the secrets he guarded so closely.

The studio was a haven of creativity, filled with vibrant canvases and intricate pieces that told stories only Ethan could fully understand. Sarah's fingers traced the strokes of his brush as if searching for hidden clues within the layers of paint.

One painting caught her attention—an intense stormy seascape dominating one studio wall. Dark clouds loomed ominously in the sky, and the waves crashed against jagged rocks with a furious intensity. It was a portrayal of turmoil and hidden depths, mirroring the uncertainty in her own heart.

Sarah couldn't tear her eyes away from the painting, feeling an inexplicable connection between the turbulent scene before her and the storm of emotions she had been navigating. It was as if the artwork held the key to unlocking the secrets that had been kept from her.

Her thoughts were interrupted when Ethan quietly entered the studio, his presence causing her to startle slightly. He watched her momentarily before speaking, his voice tinged with vulnerability and hesitation.

"Sarah," he began, his eyes locked on the stormy seascape, "that painting—it's a reflection of the battles I've faced in my past, the storms I've weathered. But it's also a reminder that even in the darkest times, there can be beauty and hope."

Sarah turned to face him, her gaze searching his eyes for answers. "Ethan, I want to understand, to be a part of your world, but I can't do that if you keep me in the dark."

Ethan sighed, his shoulders slumping as he wrestled with his internal turmoil. "Sarah, I promise I will share everything with you when ready. There are just things I need to come to terms with first."

Sarah nodded, her heart heavy with the weight of their unspoken secrets. She knew that trust took time to build, and she was willing to wait for Ethan to find the courage to reveal the truths he held within his heart.

As they stood in the studio, surrounded by the artwork that spoke of both turmoil and hope, Sarah couldn't help but hope that their love would be the beacon that guided them through the storms of their pasts toward a future filled with clarity, trust and a deeper understanding of each other. Seabreeze Bay, with its ever-watchful waves, would bear witness to their journey as they navigated the artistic dilemmas of their hearts.

Late at night, when the world outside was cloaked in the soft embrace of darkness, Sarah and Ethan often found solace in each other's company. Their shared dreams and aspirations had been the threads that wove the tapestry of their budding love story. But now, their conversations carried a weight of uncertainty, like a storm brewing on the horizon.

They would sit together, the moonlight streaming through the window, casting ethereal shadows across the room. The hushed tones of their voices filled the air, creating an intimate bubble where their thoughts and feelings could be shared without reservation.

But despite the intimacy of their late-night talks, Sarah couldn't help but question whether their love could weather the secrets that loomed between them. The unspoken truths had become a barrier she couldn't ignore, a wall between the deep connection she craved and the fear of what lay on the other side.

Ethan, too, had his doubts. He knew he needed to open up to Sarah, let her in, and reveal the hidden chapters of his past that had shaped him into the man he was today. Yet, the fear of reliving the painful memories and the vulnerability that came with it held him back.

Their late-night conversations became a battlefield of unspoken fears and desires. Each word they shared held a hidden weight, an unspoken question that hung like a delicate balance waiting to tip.

Sarah would look at Ethan with longing, desperately wanting to bridge the gap between them. But the words that needed to be said remained trapped within their hearts, like prisoners of fear and uncertainty.

Ethan would meet her gaze with a mixture of love and regret, silently wishing he could free himself from the burdens of the past and give Sarah the transparency she deserved.

In those late-night moments, as the moonlight painted their faces with silver hues, Sarah and Ethan found themselves at a crossroads. Their love was undeniable, but the secrets they kept threatened to tear them apart.

With its calming waves and healing embrace, Seabreeze Bay watched over them as they grappled with their doubts and desires, knowing that the path to true love was often paved with challenges and sacrifices.

The tension between Sarah and Ethan was palpable, like an invisible force that had settled between them. Their once effortless connection, filled with laughter and shared dreams, now seemed strained, as if a growing chasm separated them.

Every glance they exchanged held a touch of sadness as if they were mourning the simplicity of their love. Once spoken with joy and excitement, their words were tinged with the weight of unspoken doubt that had nestled in their hearts.

They longed for the days when their love was uncomplicated when they reveled in the magic of Seabreeze Bay without the looming shadows of secrets and uncertainties. But now, those shadows had seeped into their relationship, threatening to tear them apart like relentless waves eroding the shoreline.

Sarah would sometimes catch herself staring at Ethan, her heart heavy with the fear of losing the love they had found. She yearned for the reassurance of his open heart, for the transparency that would bridge the widening gap between them.

Ethan, too, felt the growing distance between them, and it weighed on him like an anchor dragging him down. He had always been a man of few words when it came to his past, but now he understood that his silence was driving a wedge between him and the woman he loved.

With its calming waves and timeless beauty, Seabreeze Bay bore witness to the turmoil within their hearts. It had been a place of healing and love, but now it stood as a silent witness to the challenges that threatened to engulf their relationship.

Sarah and Ethan knew they needed to confront the growing chasm that separated them to find a way back to the love that had once been their guiding light. But the journey to mend their fractured connection would not be easy, for it meant facing the secrets and uncertainties that had taken root in their hearts, and only time would reveal if their love could weather the storm and emerge stronger on the other side.

One evening, as the sun dipped below the horizon, casting Seabreeze Bay in shades of pink and gold, Sarah stood at a crossroads—a moment of reckoning building like an impending storm. She knew she could no longer ignore the secrets that Ethan was keeping, the unspoken doubts that had taken root in their relationship.

It was an evening when the sky seemed to mirror the turmoil in her heart, a moment when she had to confront the uncertainties that loomed on the horizon. The weight of her decision hung in the air like an unspoken truth that refused to be ignored.

Sarah had come to a heartbreaking realization—a pivotal moment where she needed to lay everything bare, to face Ethan and the secrets he held close. It was a test of their love's resilience, a challenge to see if the foundation of their relationship could withstand the storm that had gathered around them.

She couldn't bear the uncertainty any longer, the growing chasm that separated them. And so, with determination in her heart and a sense of vulnerability that made her tremble, Sarah knew she would need to make a choice.

Ethan had become a part of her heart, a piece of her soul, and she couldn't let the doubts and secrets erode what they had built together. As she prepared to face the truth and demand the transparency she desperately needed, Sarah braced herself for the consequences her decision might bring.

With its ever-watchful waves and timeless beauty, Seabreeze Bay bore witness to the pivotal moment in their love story. It was a place of healing and transformation, but now it would become the backdrop for a heart-wrenching decision that would shape the course of their love and either lead them to calmer shores or leave them in the wake of a

storm.

CHAPTER TEN: STORMY SEAS

In the heart of Seabreeze Bay, where the gentle waves whispered tales of love, Sarah and Ethan's once-blissful relationship had become entangled in a web of misunderstandings. It all started with a seemingly innocuous conversation about Sarah's upcoming photography project— a solo journey to a remote island. She had mentioned it excitedly, eager to share her plans with the man she loved, but the unexpected storm of their emotions was about to cast a shadow over their love.

They sat in their cozy living room, where the warmth of their shared love had once enveloped them. But now, the tension in the air was palpable, like a gathering stormcloud. Sarah had expected Ethan to be as excited as she was about her project, to embrace her adventurous spirit and the passion that fueled her creativity. However, his response had been quite the opposite.

Ethan's face tensed, his brows furrowing with worry as he spoke, "A remote island, Sarah? It sounds dangerous. I don't want you to go alone."

Sarah, caught off guard by his reaction, felt a mixture of frustration and disappointment wash over her. She had always been fiercely independent and unapologetically adventurous, and this sudden concern from Ethan felt suffocating, like a gust of wind snuffing out the flame of her excitement. "Ethan, I can take care of myself," she replied, her voice hinting at defiance. "It's just a photography project."

But her words seemed to escalate the tension between them, like gathering clouds before a storm. Once filled with their laughter and shared dreams, the room held an uncomfortable silence stretching endlessly. It was a silence heavy with unspoken emotions, with the weight of their contrasting desires and fears.

Ethan, who felt protective of Sarah, couldn't help but worry about her safety. He knew her determination and spirit were part of what he loved about her, but the thought of her embarking on a solo journey to a remote and potentially dangerous place gnawed at his heart.

Sarah, on the other hand, felt like her wings were being clipped just as she was ready to soar. She yearned for the freedom to explore, to capture the world's beauty through her lens, and the sudden resistance from Ethan left her feeling misunderstood and restrained.

At that moment, as the storm of their emotions raged silently between them, Sarah and Ethan found themselves on opposing shores, struggling to bridge the gap that had opened up in their once-solid foundation. Seabreeze Bay, which had borne witness to the beauty of their love, now watched as their relationship faced its greatest challenge—a storm of misunderstanding and unspoken desires that threatened to tear them apart.

Once a sanctuary of love and laughter, the cozy living room had transformed into a battleground of emotions as Sarah and Ethan's disagreement escalated into a heated argument. The air crackled with tension; their words exchanged like lightning bolts illuminating the stormy night.

Sarah, her fiery spirit ignited, felt like her hard-fought independence was being stifled by Ethan's well-intentioned but suffocating worry. Her voice quivered with frustration and determination as she cried, "Ethan, you can't control my life! I need to do this for myself, for my art. It's who I am."

Equally frustrated and concerned for her safety, Ethan couldn't contain the storm of emotions within him. His voice rose, matching the intensity of the brewing storm outside, as he shouted back, "I can't lose you, Sarah. I can't bear the thought of something happening to you. You mean everything to me."

Their love, once a source of strength, had become a turbulent sea. Its waves crashed against the rocky shores of their pride and stubbornness, each argumentative tide eroding the foundations of their relationship. The walls they had built around their hearts crumbled in the face of their conflicting desires and fears.

The room echoed with their heated words, their love now a turbulent sea, its depths filled with unspoken regrets and unresolved tensions. As the storm raged inside and outside, Sarah and Ethan were left grappling with the uncertainty of whether their love could survive this tempestuous test or if the relentless waves of their pride would sweep it away.

Outside, the world seemed to mirror the turmoil within their relationship. Once clear and serene, the sky had darkened with ominous clouds that gathered like the heavy weight of their unspoken doubts. The first drops of rain, hesitant at first, tapped against the windowpane like the gentlest of tears, mirroring the tears that streamed down Sarah's face.

As the argument between Sarah and Ethan raged on, they both noticed the sudden downpour outside. It was as if the storm within them had manifested in the world around them, the rain echoing their emotional turmoil. Each raindrop splattered against the windowpane was like an unspoken word, a reminder of the fragile nature of their love.

Sarah's voice quivered with frustration as she cried, "Ethan, you can't control my life! I need to do this for myself, for my art. It's who I am."

Ethan's face was a portrait of conflicted emotions, his eyes filled with worry as he shouted back, "I can't lose you, Sarah. I can't bear the thought of something happening to you. You mean everything to me."

Once filled with heated exchanges, the room fell into an uneasy silence as they both turned to look at the storm outside. It was a moment of reflection, a pause in the storm of their emotions, as if the universe was urging them to reconsider their positions and find a way to navigate the turbulent waters of their love.

Sarah's tears mixed with the rain, the world outside a reflection of the emotional turmoil within her heart. The sudden downpour served as a poignant reminder of the fragile balance between love and pride, a reminder that, sometimes, storms came from the skies and the depths of the human heart. Each raindrop carried the weight of their unspoken regrets and unresolved tensions, leaving them both questioning whether their love could withstand this tempestuous test or if the relentless waves of their pride would sweep it away.

As the argument continued, the storm outside intensified, mirroring the escalating disruption of emotions within the room. Lightning streaked across the sky, illuminating their faces as they clashed like opposing currents in a turbulent sea.

Sarah's internal thoughts were a whirlwind of frustration and determination. She couldn't comprehend why Ethan was trying to hold her back from pursuing her passion. She had always been fiercely independent, and this project was more than just a job; it was an opportunity to prove herself as an artist and photographer. She thought, "Why can't he see that this is important to me? I need him to trust in my abilities and understand how much this means."

Ethan, on the other hand, was struggling with his inner turmoil. He loved Sarah deeply, and the thought of something happening to her filled him with dread. He thought, "I can't lose her. She's the most precious thing in my life. But am I being too overprotective? Is my fear driving a wedge between us?"

Their love, once a source of comfort and strength, had become a battleground of conflicting desires and fears. Outside, the thunder rumbled in response to their passionate exchange, as if nature was echoing their turmoil. The room was charged with tension, their love caught in the eye of the storm, both of them grappling with the realization that their relationship was facing its most significant challenge yet.

Eventually, both Sarah and Ethan were emotionally drained. Their voices had grown hoarse from the heated exchange, and their anger had ebbed away like a receding tide. Exhaustion had replaced their initial frustration, and they were sitting in a heavy silence.

The room seemed to absorb the residual tension, and the air felt thick with the aftermath of their argument. Raindrops on the windowpane glistened like silent witnesses to their emotional turmoil, and the storm outside had subsided, leaving a quiet, reflective atmosphere in its wake.

Sarah's thoughts were a jumble of conflicting emotions. She still believed in the importance of her photography project, but she couldn't shake the feeling that her relationship with Ethan had been strained to its limits.

She wondered if they could find a way to bridge the gap that had grown between them during their argument.

Ethan, too, was lost in thought. He loved Sarah with all his heart but realized his fears had driven a wedge between them. Ethan couldn't bear the thought of losing her, but he also couldn't bear the thought of stifling her independence. He knew they needed to find a compromise, a way to trust each other while pursuing their passions.

As they sat in the quiet aftermath of the storm, Sarah and Ethan were acutely aware that their love had been tested and that they had made difficult decisions. The room, once filled with the echoes of their argument, now held the promise of resolution and understanding.

With the storm passed, Sarah and Ethan were left to pick up the pieces of their relationship. They sat in the quiet aftermath, both acutely aware that their love was worth fighting for, but it needed to weather the emerging challenges.

Ethan reached out and gently took Sarah's hand. His voice was soft with sincerity. "I'm sorry, Sarah. I worry about you because I love you so much."

Sarah nodded, tears glistening in her eyes. Her voice was filled with emotion. "And I love you too, Ethan. But I need you to trust and support me in pursuing my passion."

Their reconciliation was fragile, like the clearing skies after a fierce storm. They knew that their love had the strength to weather even the harshest of storms, but they also understood that they needed to find a way to communicate and compromise if their relationship was to survive the rocky seas ahead.

In that quiet moment, as the remnants of their argument and the echoes of the storm faded into memory, Sarah and Ethan clung to the belief that their love could overcome any obstacle. The future remained uncertain, but they were determined to navigate it together, hand in hand, as they learned to trust, compromise, and truly understand

the depths of their love for each other.

CHAPTER ELEVEN: HEARTFELT CONFESSIONS

After their argument and fragile reconciliation, Sarah and Ethan decided to take time out. They retreated to their respective spaces, needing a moment to collect their thoughts and emotions.

In her room, Sarah stared out of the window at the tranquil bay. She knew that she had to address Ethan's secrets, but she also realized that her need for independence had been a source of conflict. Her mind was a whirlwind of emotions and doubts as she prepared for a heartfelt conversation with Ethan.

Sarah took a deep breath and went to Ethan's art studio. She found him sitting in front of a blank canvas, lost in thought. The air was tense, but Sarah knew they needed to talk.

"Ethan," she began, her voice soft yet determined. "We can't keep avoiding these conversations. We must address the secrets and fears driving a wedge between us."

Ethan turned to look at her, his eyes reflecting a mixture of regret and longing. "You're right, Sarah. I've been holding back, and it's not fair to you. But there are things from my past that I've kept hidden because I thought they'd drive you away."

Sarah moved closer, taking his hand in hers. "Ethan, I love you and want to understand everything about you—the good and the bad. We can only move forward if we're honest with each other."

Tears welled up in Ethan's eyes as he nodded. "I'm just scared, Sarah. Scared of losing you."

Sarah cupped his face gently, wiping away a tear with her thumb. "You won't lose me, Ethan, as long as we face these challenges together."

Their heartfelt conversation continued late into the night as they shared their deepest fears and regrets. It was a difficult but necessary step toward healing their relationship and building a stronger foundation based on trust and open communication.

In the days that followed their heartfelt conversation, Sarah and Ethan embarked on a journey of rediscovery. They were determined to rebuild their relationship and let go of the past mistakes that had haunted them.

They spent time together, savoring the simple pleasures of Seabreeze Bay. One sunny afternoon, they packed a picnic basket and headed to their favorite spot on the beach. The warm sand beneath their toes, the soothing sound of the waves, and the taste of fresh seafood made it a perfect day. They laughed, shared stories, and allowed themselves to bask in the joy of each other's company.

Another day, they decided to explore the coastal trails, hand in hand, rediscovering the natural beauty of their hometown. The rugged cliffs, the breathtaking vistas, and the scent of the sea breeze invigorated their spirits.

In the evenings, they retreated to Ethan's art studio, where they painted together. Sarah discovered a newfound appreciation for the therapeutic nature of painting, and Ethan marveled at her talent and creativity. Their artistic collaborations became a testament to their growing bond.

Their love felt like a second chance at happiness, and they were determined not to let their past mistakes overshadow their future. They were rebuilding their relationship one moment at a time, forging a more profound connection based on trust, communication, and a shared love for Seabreeze Bay.

Trust was a fragile component of their relationship, and Sarah and Ethan knew they had to work diligently to rebuild it. They consciously tried to have open and honest conversations about their insecurities and fears, promising to communicate and support each other through thick and thin consistently.

But the path to trust was not without its challenges. There were moments of doubt and uncertainty, like navigating a treacherous sea. Sarah sometimes questioned whether Ethan was keeping more secrets, and Ethan, in turn, doubted Sarah's need for independence.

One evening, as they sat on their favorite bench overlooking the bay, Sarah admitted her doubts. "Ethan, I can't help but wonder if there's anything else you're not telling me. Can I trust that you've shared everything?"

Ethan looked into her eyes, his gaze unwavering. "Sarah, I promise I've shared everything relevant to us. There are painful memories from my past that I haven't talked about, but they don't affect our relationship."

Sarah nodded, understanding that some wounds might take time to heal. "And I promise, Ethan, to be more open about my plans and dreams. We're a team, and I want you to be a part of every aspect of my life."

Their commitment to trust was a continual effort, but they faced each challenge together. In these moments of vulnerability and reassurance, their love grew more substantial, like a ship navigating rough waters and emerging even more resilient on the other side.

Following their argument and heartfelt confessions, they both realized the importance of working on their relationship and addressing their insecurities and fears. They wanted to put the past behind them and focus on nurturing their love.

Understanding the significance of trust and communication, Ethan decided to plan a romantic surprise for Sarah. He knew that sharing a unique, intimate dinner would be a meaningful way to reaffirm their commitment to each other.

So, he secretly made reservations at the seaside restaurant, which held sentimental value for both of them. It was a restaurant they had visited in the early stages of their relationship when everything had felt easy and filled with promise. Ethan wanted to recreate that magic and remind Sarah of their love for each other.

When he revealed his surprise to Sarah, she was deeply moved by the gesture and the effort he had put into planning the evening. It became a symbol of their renewed commitment to each other, a way to rekindle the spark that had brought them together in the first place.

Thus, their visit to the restaurant was a deliberate choice made by Ethan to create a beautiful and memorable moment in their journey toward reconciliation and lasting love.

As the sun dipped below the horizon, casting a warm, golden glow across the beach, Sarah and Ethan sat at their beautifully set table. The aroma of their favorite dishes filled the air, and the flickering candles created an intimate atmosphere.

Ethan raised his glass, a soft smile playing on his lips. "To us," he toasted, his eyes locking onto Sarah's.

Sarah clinked her glass against his, her heart swelling with emotion. "To us," she echoed, her voice filled with love.

They began to dine, savoring each bite as they engaged in light conversation. The waves provided a soothing backdrop to their words, a reminder of their deep connection with Seabreeze Bay and each other.

"I wanted this to be a special evening," Ethan admitted, his eyes never leaving Sarah's. "To show you how much you mean to me."

Touched by his words, Sarah reached across the table and placed her hand over his. "It's more special than I could have ever imagined, Ethan. I love you."

Ethan's heart swelled with happiness as he squeezed her hand gently. "I love you too, Sarah. And I promise to do everything I can to make you happy."

Under the fading light of the sun and the soft glow of candlelight, they shared a moment of pure, unspoken connection. It was a romantic gesture that spoke volumes, reaffirming their love and commitment to each other, and it was a memory they would treasure for the rest of their lives.

After rekindling the romance with a romantic seaside dinner, they found themselves drawn to the beach.

Their footsteps left imprints in the soft sand as they strolled along the shoreline, the sound of crashing waves serenading their every step.

Under the canvas of a starlit sky, Sarah and Ethan found solace in the quiet beauty of the night. They lay side by side on a blanket Ethan had brought along, their fingers entwined, as they shared their dreams for the future. It was a moment of vulnerability and honesty, where they could lay bare their deepest desires and aspirations.

Ethan spoke first, his voice soft and filled with hope. "Sarah, I dream of creating art that touches people's hearts, that speaks to their souls. I want to paint the world as I see it, with all its beauty and imperfections."

Sarah turned her head to look at him, her heart swelling with affection. "And I dream of capturing those moments of raw emotion with my camera. I want to tell stories through my photography, to make people feel powerful when they see my work."

Their dreams were like stars in the night sky, distant but shining brightly with potential. They talked about the life they wanted to build together, envisioning a future where their artistic passions intertwined and fueled their love.

Ethan smiled, his gaze fixed on the stars above. "I want us to travel the world, to seek inspiration in every corner of the earth, and to create art that reflects our shared experiences."

Sarah squeezed his hand, her eyes filled with love and determination. "And I want us to face every challenge together, to navigate the storms as a team, and to cherish every beautiful moment we create."

Their shared dreams became a binding promise, a reminder that no matter what lay ahead, they would always have each other and the love that burned brightly between them under the starry night sky.

Beneath the twinkling canopy of stars, Sarah and Ethan held each other in a tender embrace. The sea whispers kissed the shore in rhythm with their hearts as they made promises that would shape their future together.

Sarah's voice, filled with sincerity, broke the silence. "Ethan, I promise always to trust you, to let you in completely. No more doubts or secrets."

Ethan gazed into her eyes, his own filled with love and determination. "And I promise to be more open with you, to share my past, fears, and dreams. You're the love of my life, Sarah, and I want us to face everything together."

Their promises hung in the air, binding them in a pact of love and devotion. The first light of dawn approached, but time seemed to stand still. With its endless horizons and healing embrace, Seabreeze Bay had become the backdrop to their love story—a story of second chances and the belief that they could weather any storm together.

CHAPTER TWELVE: A SECOND CHANCE

Sarah and Ethan's renewed connection offered hope and warmth. They decided to begin with a picnic on the beach, a simple yet meaningful way to celebrate their fresh start.

The sun bathed Seabreeze Bay's shoreline in a golden glow as Sarah and Ethan spread out their picnic blanket. They had packed a basket with sandwiches, fresh fruit, and a bottle of sparkling cider. Seagulls called out overhead, and the distant sound of waves crashing on the shore provided the perfect soundtrack.

Ethan smiled as he placed a sandwich on Sarah's plate. "I have to say, this is the best spot in town for a picnic."

Sarah chuckled and took a sip of cider. "You're not wrong, Ethan. It's as if the bay itself is celebrating our fresh start."

As they enjoyed their meal, Sarah looked at Ethan, her heart full of gratitude. "Ethan, I can't believe we almost let our doubts tear us apart."

Ethan reached for her hand, his gaze locked onto hers. "I know, Sarah. I'm thankful we found our way back to each other. This place, Seabreeze Bay, feels meant to heal us."

Their fingers intertwined, and they gazed out at the endless expanse of the sea, knowing that each day was a chance to write a new chapter in their love story.

A few days later, Sarah and Ethan decided to explore the rugged coastal trails that hugged Seabreeze Bay. They donned comfortable hiking gear and set out on an adventure.

The trail led them to breathtaking vistas where they could see the bay from different angles. The salty breeze ruffled their hair, and they couldn't help but feel invigorated by the natural beauty surrounding them.

Ethan took a moment to capture the scenery with his camera to capture scenes for later painting, and Sarah watched him with admiration. " Ethan, your passion for art makes even the simplest moments extraordinary."

Ethan chuckled, his eyes never leaving the viewfinder. "Well, that's because everything becomes extraordinary when you're in it, Sarah."

The words hung in the air, and they shared a tender moment, realizing their love could turn everyday moments into cherished memories.

Ethan's art studio had become a sanctuary for both of them. Armed with her camera, Sarah loved capturing the play of light and color on canvas as Ethan painted.

One afternoon, they sat side by side, each absorbed in their creative process. Sarah looked at Ethan's work, admiring how he brought Seabreeze Bay's beauty to life on his canvas.

She leaned over and kissed his cheek. "You know, Ethan, your art has a way of capturing the soul of this place. It's like you're sharing its secrets with the world."

Ethan set his paintbrush aside and turned to Sarah, his eyes filled with affection. "And you, Sarah, capture every moment's soul with your camera. Together, we make magic."

Their love for each other and their shared appreciation for the world around them made each moment in the art studio feel like a dance of creativity and connection.

With every passing day, Sarah and Ethan grew closer, their bond strengthened by their shared experiences and commitment to building a future together. Seabreeze Bay had become the backdrop to their rediscovery, where they could leave behind the shadows of doubt and embrace the warmth of their love.

Sarah and Ethan sat on the cozy couch in Ethan's living room, a sense of vulnerability hanging in the air. They had realized that trust was the cornerstone of their relationship, and they needed to address the doubts and insecurities that had previously strained their bond.

Sarah sighed, her gaze fixed on Ethan's. "Ethan, I want us to trust each other completely, but sometimes, my mind wanders to your secrets."

Ethan nodded, his expression filled with understanding. "I know, Sarah. And I promise I'll share everything with you when I'm ready. It's not that I don't trust you; it's just that my past is complicated."

Sarah placed her hand on his, offering reassurance. "I get that, Ethan. And I'll be patient, but I also need you to understand that keeping secrets makes it hard for me to trust completely."

They knew the path to rebuilding trust was delicate, but they were determined to navigate it together, no matter how challenging.

In the days that followed their heartfelt conversation, Sarah and Ethan had moments of doubt and insecurity. Sarah sometimes questioned whether she was being too pushy about the secrets Ethan guarded while Ethan grappled with his fears of opening up.

One evening, they decided to walk along the beach, hand in hand, their silhouettes dancing against the fading light of the day.

Sarah broke the silence, her voice gentle. "Ethan, I don't want to pressure you into sharing something you're not ready for."

Ethan squeezed her hand, his eyes filled with gratitude. "Sarah, I appreciate your patience and understanding. It's hard to open up about things from my past."

As they continued their walk, they knew that trust could not be built overnight. It required time, patience, and unwavering support. But they were committed to facing their insecurities head-on, knowing that the love they shared was worth the effort.

One evening, as they sat on their porch, watching the sun dip below the horizon, Sarah spoke from her heart. "Ethan, we've been through so much, and we've come a long way. I think the key to our trust lies in our communication."

Ethan nodded, his eyes locked onto hers. "You're right, Sarah. We must be honest, even if it's difficult."

They made a promise to each other under the fading light of the day—a promise to communicate, no matter how challenging the conversation might be. They knew that trust was fragile, but with their commitment to openness and support, they were determined to rebuild it more robustly.

Their journey was far from over, but Sarah and Ethan faced it with renewed determination and a deep love that had proven capable of weathering even the most turbulent storms.

CHAPTER THIRTEEN: LOVE'S CHALLENGES

The bright morning sun cast dappled shadows through the swaying palm trees as Mark stood on the doorstep of Sarah's cozy cottage. He had found a crumpled flyer for the Seabreeze Bay art show tucked inside a local café's bulletin board and knew she was back in her hometown.

After a few discreet inquiries around the small coastal community, he had tracked down her address. Mark's heart raced with hope and trepidation as he rehearsed his words.

His knock echoed through the tranquil surroundings, and when the door opened, Sarah's surprised expression met his determined one.

"Mark?" She blinked, taken aback.

"Sarah," he said, his voice carrying a hint of vulnerability he had rarely shown before, "I've thought about us a lot, and I can't just let you go like this. Can we talk?"

Sarah glanced back into her cottage, her solitude giving her pause. She knew she had moved on from her past relationship with Mark, but his unexpected appearance threatened to disrupt the newfound happiness she had found in Seabreeze Bay.

After internal deliberation, she nodded and replied to Mark, "Okay, let's talk. But how about we meet at the diner on the outskirts of town? I need to put some fuel in my car, and it's quieter there."

Mark agreed although he couldn't help but wonder why she wanted to keep their meeting away from the town center. As they walked toward their respective cars, a cloud of uncertainty hung in the air, threatening to disrupt the tranquility of their seaside paradise.

Sarah and Mark drove separately to the quaint diner on the outskirts of Seabreeze Bay. The road stretched ahead, flanked by tall trees on either side, their leaves rustling in the gentle coastal breeze. Sarah kept her eyes on the road, her hands gripping the steering wheel with apprehension.

As they arrived and parked their cars, they entered the cozy diner. The scent of freshly brewed coffee and sizzling bacon greeted them as they found an empty booth by the window, casting a view of the sparkling ocean in the distance.

Sarah ordered a coffee and a simple breakfast, her appetite curbed by the weight of the conversation. Mark followed suit, trying to hide his nervousness behind a veneer of composure.

They sat in tense silence once their orders had been placed, staring at the tranquil seascape beyond the window. The waves whispered secrets to the shore, mirroring their unspoken words.

Finally, Sarah spoke, her voice soft but determined, "Mark, I appreciate you coming here, but I want to be clear. My life has moved on, and I've found happiness in Seabreeze Bay."

Mark nodded, his gaze fixed on his coffee cup. "I know I made mistakes in the past, Sarah. I regret how things ended between us. I'm willing to change, to work on us."

Sarah took a deep breath, her fingers tracing the rim of her coffee cup. "Mark, this isn't about us anymore. I've started a new chapter of my life here. I've found someone who cares about me and who I care about deeply. I don't want to disrupt that."

Mark's face fell, and he looked down, his words heavy with defeat. "Is there someone else?"

Sarah hesitated for a moment, wrestling with her own emotions. Finally, she nodded. "Yes, there is. I've met someone here, and he's become very important to me."

The weight of Sarah's words settled between them, a stark reminder of the distance that had grown between their shared past and their separate futures. As they finished their breakfast in solemn silence, the waves outside continued their rhythmic dance, echoing the emotions that churned within the diner.

The minutes ticked away as Sarah and Mark grappled with their situation's reality. Mark finally broke the silence, his voice tinged with resignation.

"I see," he said, his gaze still fixed on the remnants of his breakfast. "I didn't expect things to change so much."

Sarah felt a pang of guilt for the hurt she knew she was causing him. She placed her hand gently on his, trying to offer some solace. "Mark, I want you to find happiness too, but it can't be with me. I hope you understand."

He looked up at her, his eyes filled with sadness and understanding. "I do, Sarah. I just needed to hear it from you."

They finished their coffee in quiet contemplation, the weight of their past and the uncertainty of their futures lingering like a heavy fog. When the check arrived, they paid their bills, knowing it might be the last time they shared a meal.

As they exited the diner, the sun hung higher in the sky, casting a warm glow over the coastal town. Sarah and Mark exchanged a final, bittersweet glance before going their separate ways, each on their path to healing and happiness.

That evening, when Sarah returned to her cottage, she couldn't shake the weight of the meeting with Mark. She knew she needed to be honest with Ethan, to tell him about her past and the unexpected encounter. After all, they had promised each other transparency and trust.

Sarah invited Ethan over for the evening; as they sat down for dinner, the soft candlelight casting a warm glow over the room, Sarah finally broached the topic. "Ethan, I need to tell you something," she began cautiously.

Ethan looked up from his plate, his curiosity piqued. "What is it, Sarah?"

She took a deep breath, her eyes meeting his. "Mark, my ex-boyfriend, he showed up today. He saw the flyer for our art show and found out I was back in Seabreeze Bay. He wanted to talk, so we met for coffee this morning."

Ethan's reaction was not what Sarah had anticipated. His face contorted with jealousy and rage, his voice rising as he struggled to control his emotions. "You met him without telling me first? What else aren't you telling me, Sarah?"

His explosive reaction took Sarah aback. She hadn't expected him to be thrilled about the meeting, but she hadn't anticipated this level of anger either. "Ethan, it was just a conversation. I told him about us, about our relationship."

Ethan pushed his plate away, his frustration evident. "And what else did you two talk about, Sarah? Do I need to worry that he will show up again?"

Sarah felt a mixture of frustration and hurt. "Ethan, there's nothing more to it. I promise. I didn't tell you immediately because I didn't want to upset you."

But Ethan's jealousy had ignited a fire within him, and he couldn't quiet it. "Upset me? It would help if you had been upfront with me from the start, Sarah. Secrets have no place in our relationship."

"You're one to talk; you keep more secrets and never let me in," Sarah exclaimed.

Their dinner had turned into a battlefield of emotions, and the once romantic atmosphere had soured. Sarah realized their once strong and unwavering love was now facing another test that threatened to push them to their limits.

Sarah and Ethan's heated exchange continued to escalate like a stormy sea crashing against the rocky shores of their relationship. Each word they hurled at each other felt like another wave, eroding the trust and understanding they had painstakingly built.

Ethan's anger was relentless. "Sarah, I can't believe you'd meet with your ex behind my back. You don't trust me enough to tell me what's happening."

Sarah, feeling cornered, fired back, "This isn't about trust, Ethan. It's about my past, which has nothing to do with us."

Ethan shook his head, his frustration evident. "Everything from your past affects us now, Sarah. You should have considered how it might make me feel."

Their voices rose higher, their argument echoing through the cottage. Sarah felt regretful for not handling the situation differently but refused to back down entirely. "Ethan, you need to trust me too. I chose you, and I'm with you because I love you."

Ethan's expression softened, and he sighed, his anger giving way to sadness. "I know, Sarah. I can't help but feel threatened when your past comes back like this."

Sarah touched Ethan's hand, trying to bridge their widening emotional gap. "Ethan, I love you and want us to work through this. We can't let jealousy and anger tear us apart."

Ethan looked into her eyes, the storm of emotions subsiding. "You're right, Sarah. I love you, too, and I don't want to lose what we have. But we need to be open and honest with each other, no matter how difficult it may be."

Their argument had left them both emotionally drained, but in its wake, they had a chance to rebuild their trust more than before. They knew that love could weather even the fiercest storms if they were willing to face their challenges together.

As they held each other close that night, the wounds of their argument slowly began to heal, and their love emerged from the turmoil stronger and more resilient.

The following afternoon, the gentle lapping of the waves against the shore provided a soothing backdrop as Sarah and Ethan stood on the beach, the sun sinking lower on the horizon. The weight of their recent argument had hung heavily in the air, but now, there was hope in this moment of reconciliation.

Sarah spoke first, her voice shaky with emotion. "Ethan, I'm so sorry for meeting with Mark without telling you. It was wrong, and I should have been more transparent with you."

Ethan nodded, his own eyes glistening with unshed tears. "I'm sorry too, Sarah, for reacting as I did. I should have trusted you more."

Their heartfelt apologies washed away the lingering tension, and they reached for each other, their arms wrapping around in a tight embrace. The tears they had held back during their argument now flowed freely, cleansing their souls of the hurt and misunderstandings.

Ethan kissed Sarah's forehead, his voice filled with sincerity. "I love you, Sarah, more than anything. I don't want anything to come between us."

Sarah nodded, tears trickling down her cheeks. "I love you too, Ethan. I want us to be strong, to trust each other completely."

As the sun dipped below the horizon, they stood together on the beach, knowing that their love was like the eternal ebb and flow of the tides—firm, unyielding, and ready to weather any storm that came their way. Their reconciliation was a testament to the resilience of their love, a bond that had only grown stronger through the trials they had faced.

With renewed commitment and a deeper understanding of each other's fears and vulnerabilities, they walked hand in hand back to their cottage, ready to face whatever challenges lay ahead.

In the days following Mark's initial visit, he persisted in his attempts to contact Sarah. Late-night texts and voicemails flooded her phone, creating an unwelcome intrusion into her peaceful life with Ethan in Seabreeze Bay.

One evening, as Sarah sat with Ethan on their favorite bench overlooking the bay, she couldn't ignore the persistent buzzing of her phone in her bag. With a sigh, she retrieved it and saw a string of messages from Mark. She couldn't bear the thought of dealing with this alone any longer. She needed Ethan's support, his presence to face Mark and finally put an end to this intrusion.

"Ethan," she said, her voice tinged with frustration, "Mark won't stop. He's been sending me texts and calling me non-stop."

Ethan, his brows furrowing with concern, glanced at the messages. "Sarah, we need to deal with this together. Let's meet him, and I'll be right there with you."

Sarah nodded, relief washing over her. She knew facing Mark with Ethan by her side would make all the difference. They planned to meet Mark at a local café, a neutral ground where Sarah could clarify her feelings.

With the weight of Ethan's support, Sarah finally felt ready to confront Mark and end the disruption he had brought into their lives. She knew their love was more substantial than any external force, and together, they would face this challenge head-on.

The café was bathed in the soft glow of evening when Sarah, Ethan, and Mark sat down together at a corner table. Mark had recently gone through a breakup, and the sting of loneliness had led him back to Seabreeze Bay, where he thought he could rekindle what he had once shared with

Sarah. However, he sensed Sarah's request's urgency and finally agreed to meet them.

Resting firmly on Ethan's, Sarah took a deep breath and looked at Mark with unwavering resolve. "Mark, I need you to understand something. I've moved on, and I'm deeply in love with Ethan. I want you to respect that and leave Seabreeze Bay for good."

Mark, his eyes fixed on Sarah, nodded slowly. The pain of his recent breakup was still fresh in his mind, but he now recognized that Sarah had moved on, and there was no going back. He turned to Ethan, his expression sincere. "Take care of her, Ethan. She deserves someone who can make her happy."

Ethan nodded in response, a sense of relief washing over him. He had been prepared to protect his relationship with Sarah, but Mark's willingness to let go diffused the tension in the air.

Sarah reached across the table, placing her hand on Mark's for a brief moment. "Thank you for understanding, Mark. I wish you all the best."

With that, Mark stood up, leaving some money on the table for his untouched coffee. He looked at them one last time and then walked out of the café, disappearing into the fading light of the evening.

As the door swung shut behind Mark, Sarah turned to Ethan, her eyes filled with gratitude and love. They knew that this moment had solidified their bond and removed the last obstacle standing in the way of their love. With a shared smile, they left the café hand in hand, ready to face their future with renewed strength and hope.

As they walked back to their cozy cottage by the bay, Sarah and Ethan felt a weight lift from their shoulders. The air was filled with a sense of peace and a newfound appreciation for the strength of their love.

Ethan squeezed Sarah's hand gently, his voice filled with warmth. "I'm so proud of you, Sarah. You handled that with grace and strength."

Sarah smiled up at him, her heart brimming with love. "It's because of you, Ethan. Your trust and support mean everything to me."

They reached their cottage and sat on the porch, the sound of waves in the background providing a soothing backdrop to their conversation. They turned their focus to the future with the challenging chapter behind them.

Ethan spoke softly, his eyes locked onto Sarah's. "I promise to always be open with you, never to let doubt come between us."

Sarah leaned in and kissed him, sealing their promise. "And I promise to cherish what we have and never let anything or anyone come between us."

Under the starry Seabreeze Bay sky, Sarah and Ethan found solace in each other's arms, grateful for the challenges they had overcome and the love that had grown stronger because of them.

CHAPTER FOURTEEN: SECRETS UNVEILED

The morning sun streamed through the windows of Sarah's cozy cottage in Seabreeze Bay. Sarah had prepared a special breakfast, and the table was set with care, but a lingering doubt cast a shadow over the morning for her.

Ethan arrived on time, his smile warm, and he kissed Sarah gently. "Morning, love. What's this?" he asked, taking in the delicious food before him.

As they sat down for their morning meal, the clinking of utensils against plates was the only sound in the room. Sarah couldn't help but steal glances at Ethan, her curiosity gnawing at her like an itch she couldn't scratch.

"Ethan," she began tentatively, her voice soft, "there's something I've wanted to talk to you about."

Ethan, who had been sipping his coffee, looked up, his expression guarded. "What is it, Sarah?"

"I've noticed something on your mind," she said carefully. "You've been distant lately, and it worries me."

Ethan's brows furrowed, and he sighed and set his coffee mug down. "It's nothing, Sarah. Just work stuff. You know how it gets sometimes."

But Sarah wasn't convinced. She had seen how his eyes clouded with unease when he thought she wasn't looking. "Ethan, I want to be there for you," she said, her voice filled with concern. "We promised to share everything, remember?"

Ethan's defenses went up instantly, and he bristled at her words. "I don't need you prying into my business, Sarah. Some things are better left alone."

The tension in the room was palpable, and their once tranquil breakfast had turned into a battleground of words. Sarah felt a knot forming in her stomach as they exchanged heated words, their frustration driving a wedge between them.

Their argument escalated like a brewing storm on the horizon. Sarah's concern had grown into a gnawing ache that she couldn't ignore, and Ethan's defensiveness only fueled her determination to uncover his secret.

"Ethan, this isn't about prying," Sarah insisted, her voice shaking with emotion. "I just want to understand what's been bothering you. We promised to be open with each other."

Ethan's jaw clenched, and he pushed his plate away, his appetite lost in the turmoil of their conversation. "Sarah, there are things in my past that I'd rather not bring up. It has nothing to do with us."

Sarah's heart ached as she watched the man she loved retreat behind a wall of silence. "Ethan, when we started this relationship, we agreed that our pasts wouldn't haunt us. We promised to face everything together."

Ethan's frustration boiled over, and he stood abruptly, knocking his chair back. "I need some air," he muttered before storming out of the cottage, leaving Sarah alone at the table.

As Sarah watched him go, her heart heavy with worry and uncertainty, she couldn't help but wonder if their love was strong enough to weather this storm. The secrets that loomed between them threatened to tear their relationship apart, and the desire to uncover the truth battled with her fear of pushing Ethan away further.

Sarah couldn't bear the distance that had grown between her and Ethan. The need to uncover his secret had become a relentless itch in her mind, and she knew she had to find answers.

While Ethan was out, Sarah ducked down to the studio, searching for clues or hints about what he was hiding. She combed through drawers, peeked into notebooks, and even checked the messages on his calendar.

Her heart raced as she dug deeper into his life, feeling guilty for invading his privacy but unable to ignore her growing concern. Every unopened letter, every hidden photo, and every cryptic message fueled her determination to unravel the mystery.

Ethan returned to Sarah's cottage later that day, their tension still simmering beneath the surface. Sarah's desperate search had yielded no concrete answers, but her unease had only grown.

As he walked in, Sarah couldn't contain her frustration any longer. "Ethan, we need to talk about this," she implored, her voice trembling.

Ethan sighed wearily, his shoulders slumping. "Sarah, can we please drop it? I told you, it's nothing."

But Sarah couldn't drop it. The uncertainty was eating away at her, and she needed to know the truth. "Ethan, I love you, and I'm terrified that whatever you keep from me will destroy us. Please, tell me."

Their eyes locked in a battle of wills, and Sarah's heart ached as she saw the torment in Ethan's gaze. The silence that followed was heavy, filled with the weight of their unspoken fears and desires.

The tension in their cottage had reached a breaking point. Sarah's desperate need for answers clashed with Ethan's stubborn silence, and their love, once a source of strength, had become a battleground.

Sarah felt her emotions overwhelming her, tears streaming down her cheeks as she faced the man she loved. "Ethan, please," she pleaded, her voice breaking, "I can't keep going like this. I need to know the truth."

Ethan, his own emotions raw and exposed, finally relented. He slumped onto a chair, his head in his hands. "Sarah, you have to understand. There are things I have tried to leave behind."

Sarah moved closer to him, her heart aching with empathy. "Ethan, whatever it is, we can face it together. I don't care about your past; I only care about us."

The truth spilled out like a long-kept confession as Ethan finally opened up. He took a deep breath, his voice trembling with relief and vulnerability. Sarah sat across from him, her eyes filled with empathy, her hand gently resting on his.

Ethan's gaze was distant as he began, "Sarah, there's something I've been keeping from you. It's about someone from my past—someone I loved deeply."

Sarah tightened her grip on his hand, silently encouraging him to continue. "His name was Daniel," Ethan continued, his voice filled with a bittersweet ache. "We were together for years, and he was the love of my life."

As he spoke, tears welled in Ethan's eyes, his memories flooding with pain. "We were planning our future together, Sarah. We had dreams of traveling, of seeing the world. But then... then he got sick."

Sarah felt her heartache for Ethan as she listened. "Ethan, I'm so sorry," she whispered, her voice filled with compassion.

Ethan nodded, his emotions threatening to overwhelm him. "I watched him suffer, Sarah, and I couldn't do anything to help him. It was the most helpless I've ever felt in my life."

He wiped away a tear that had escaped, and then he continued. "Daniel passed away, and it shattered me. I... I couldn't bear the pain, so I left everything behind and came to Seabreeze Bay to heal."

Sarah's eyes glistened with tears as she took in the weight of Ethan's confession. "Ethan, I can't imagine how difficult that must have been for you."

Ethan nodded, his voice still trembling. "I never thought I could love again, Sarah. But then you came into my life and showed me that it was possible to find happiness and love again."

As the truth of Ethan's past unfolded, Sarah felt a deep sense of understanding and connection with him. She realized that his secrets had been a shield to protect himself from the pain of his past, and her love and support were helping him heal.

Their conversation continued late into the night, with Ethan sharing more about Daniel and their planned life. Sarah listened with an open heart, feeling closer to Ethan than ever. He feared she wouldn't accept his bi-sexual past. The weight of his secret had been lifted, and the healing process had truly begun.

The dawn sun cast a warm, forgiving light over Sarah and Ethan as they sat on the porch of their cottage. The truth had been laid bare, and their relationship had reached a fragile but vital turning point.

Ethan's secret, once a shadow looming over their love, had lost its power. Sarah's unwavering support and understanding had brought them closer together, and the wounds that had festered in their hearts were beginning to heal.

They held hands, intertwined fingers, and gazed at the tranquil bay. The silence between them was no longer filled with tension but with a sense of renewed hope.

The path ahead would still be challenging, but they were ready to face it together, armed with the love that had weathered the storm of secrets.

Their fragile reconciliation was a testament to the strength of their love, a love that had endured despite the doubts, fears, and uncertainties that had threatened to tear them apart.

CHAPTER FIFTEEN: REBUILDING THE BOND

The first rays of the morning sun filtered through the curtains of Sarah's cozy Seabreeze Bay cottage. She stirred, feeling the warmth of the sun on her face. Her gaze shifted to the bedside clock; it was almost time.

A soft knock on the door followed, and she knew who it was. She couldn't help but smile as she exited the bed and threw on a robe. Her heart raced with anticipation.

When Sarah opened the door, Ethan filled the doorway with warmth and affection. His smile mirrored her as he greeted her tenderly, "Good morning."

"Good morning," Sarah replied, her voice soft with affection. When Ethan visited her each morning, these moments had become a cherished part of their rekindled relationship.

They moved around the kitchen with the ease of a shared routine. Sarah set out plates while Ethan brewed a fresh pot of coffee. Their hands brushed as they passed ingredients and utensils back and forth, their morning dance a testament to their growing connection.

Once breakfast was ready, they sat down at the small dining table by the window. The view of the bay was breathtaking, the calm waters glistening in the morning light. Sarah reached across the table to hold Ethan's hand, her fingers intertwining with his.

Their conversation flowed easily, filled with laughter and shared dreams.

"Ethan," Sarah began, her gaze locked with his, "I can't believe how much better things are between us now. It's like we're building something beautiful all over again."

Ethan nodded, his eyes filled with warmth and sincerity. "I know, Sarah. I'm so grateful for this second chance, for you giving me another opportunity to be a part of your life."

Sarah squeezed his hand, a loving smile on her lips. "I couldn't imagine my life without you in it. I love you for who you are and don't feel anything negative about your past choices. These mornings with you mean everything to me."

As they sipped their coffee and exchanged morning kisses, it was clear that the simple act of being together each morning reaffirmed their rekindled love.

Sarah knew rebuilding their bond would take time, but mornings like these gave her hope. Their love was resilient, and each day brought them closer to the future they had always dreamed of.

With breakfast done and their hearts warmed by their morning routine, Sarah and Ethan decided to spend the day by the sea. It was a sunny day that made Seabreeze Bay even more enchanting.

They drove to a secluded spot by the beach, where the golden sands stretched as far as the eye could see. The rhythmic sound of the waves greeted them, a soothing melody that had become the soundtrack of their love story.

Sarah spread out a blanket while Ethan set up an umbrella for shade. They settled down on the sand, Sarah leaning against Ethan's chest as they gazed out at the vast expanse of the ocean.

Ethan's arms wrapped around her, pulling her closer. "You know, this place has always been magical for me," he said, his voice filled with nostalgia and contentment.

Sarah turned her head to look at him, her eyes curious. "How so?"

Ethan smiled, his gaze fixed on the horizon. "The beach was where I first fell in love years ago. I never thought I'd find that connection again until you came back into my life."

Sarah's heart swelled with emotion. She felt privileged to be part of this place's beautiful memories for him. "I'm glad I could be here with you," she whispered, kissing him softly.

They spent the day walking along the shore, their fingers entwined. They collected seashells, shared stories, and basked in the warm sun. With every step they took, their bond grew more substantial, and the doubts and insecurities of the past felt like distant echoes.

As the day turned into evening, they sat side by side on the beach, watching the sun dip below the horizon. The colors of the sky shifted from vibrant blues to warm oranges and pinks, painting a breathtaking scene.

Ethan turned to Sarah, his eyes filled with a deep, unwavering affection. "Sarah, I want you to know I'm committed to making this work for us."

Sarah met his gaze, her heart skipping a beat. "I feel the same way, Ethan. I believe in us."

With the sun below the horizon, they stayed on the beach, wrapped in each other's arms. The sea whispered its secrets to them, and the stars above shone brighter as if celebrating their love.

At that moment, by the sea they both cherished, Sarah and Ethan knew their love was rekindled and stronger than ever.

The art studio, a sanctuary of creativity and intimacy, became the backdrop for a profoundly vulnerable conversation between Sarah and Ethan. Surrounded by the tools of their respective crafts, they found solace in each other's presence.

Sarah's eyes shimmered with unshed tears as she began to speak, her voice trembling with vulnerability. "Ethan, there's something I've been afraid to admit. I fear losing you. I know we've had our struggles, and it scares me to think about what life would be like without you."

Ethan gazed at her with a mixture of tenderness and understanding. He reached out to caress her cheek, wiping away a single teardrop that had escaped. "Sarah, I promise you that I'm not going anywhere. I love you, and I'm here for the long haul."

Sarah nodded, her heart eased by his reassuring words. She knew their love was strong, but sometimes, the weight of past scars and uncertainties crept into her thoughts.

Feeling the weight of his vulnerability, Ethan took a deep breath before speaking. "There's something I need to share with you, Sarah. It's about my past, about someone I loved deeply."

Sarah's curiosity piqued, and she gave him her full attention. "Tell me, Ethan. I want to know."

Ethan's gaze shifted, his eyes distant as he spoke. "His name was Daniel. We were deeply in love, planning a life together. But he left, Sarah. It was such a loss, and it left me shattered."

Sarah felt a lump form in her throat as she listened to Ethan's painful revelation. She took his hand, squeezing it gently to offer her support.

Ethan continued, his voice raw with emotion. "I've carried that grief with me, and it's made me hesitant to open up to someone else fully. But being with you, Sarah has shown me that love can be a source of healing, not just pain."

Tears welled in Sarah's eyes as she realized the depth of Ethan's pain and the strength it must have taken for him to share it with her. "Ethan, I'm so sorry for your loss. Thank you for trusting me with this part of your past."

Ethan offered her a small but heartfelt smile. "Thank you for being understanding, Sarah. You mean the world to me, and I want us to build a beautiful future together."

Their vulnerable exchange had opened a new chapter in their relationship, where they could share their deepest fears and past wounds without judgment. As they held each other close in the quiet of the art studio, their connection grew, fortified by the power of their shared vulnerability and the love that bound them together.

The night was still, and the stars overhead twinkled like diamonds as Ethan set up his guitar on the beach. He had a surprise in store for Sarah that would express his love and gratitude for the second chance they had been given.

As Sarah joined him on the beach, her curiosity piqued, Ethan began to strum the guitar gently. The notes danced in the sea breeze, creating a melody that harmonized with the waves washing ashore. He sang with a voice filled with emotion:

♪ "In the moon's tender light, we found our way. Through the storms and the tears, we vowed to stay. Our love, a wild and free journey In Seabreeze Bay, where our hearts found the key.

Oh, the trials we've faced, the secrets we've shared. In each other's arms, we found how much we cared. Through every doubt and fear, we held on tight. In the darkest of nights, you were my guiding light.

So let this serenade in the starry night Be a testament to our love's endless flight. Through all the seasons, come what may, Forever, in Seabreeze Bay, our love will stay." ♪

As Ethan's song came to a gentle close, the beach seemed to hold its breath. Sarah, her eyes glistening with tears of joy, was momentarily speechless. The serenade had touched her heart in ways words couldn't express. She rushed into Ethan's arms, and they shared a sweet, passionate kiss under the starlit sky.

After the serenade, as they lay on a blanket under the moonlight, Sarah and Ethan talked about their future together. Their challenges had only deepened their love and commitment to each other.

Ethan whispered, his voice filled with sincerity, "Sarah, I promise always to be there for you, to share my joys and sorrows, and to cherish every moment we have together."

Sarah looked into his eyes, her heart filled with love. "And I promise to stand by your side, to be your rock, and to love you unconditionally. Together, we can face anything, Ethan."

With their promises made under the moon's watchful gaze, Sarah and Ethan sealed their renewed commitment with a tender kiss. Their love had weathered the storms and emerged stronger, ready to embrace the future together in Seabreeze Bay, where their hearts had found their true home.

CHAPTER SIXTEEN: A LIGHTHOUSE PROPOSAL

Sarah and Ethan decided to spend a sunny day exploring the picturesque spots that Seabreeze Bay had to offer. The weather was perfect, with a gentle breeze and a clear blue sky. They had packed a picnic basket and set out on some adventure together.

They began their day with a visit to Seabreeze Bay's famous lighthouse. It stood tall and proud, overlooking the breathtaking coastline. Sarah's camera was in hand, ready to capture the moment's beauty.

As they climbed to the top, hand in hand, their laughter filled the air. Sarah couldn't help but feel grateful for this second chance at love. She glanced at Ethan, his eyes filled with warmth and affection, and knew she was exactly where she was meant to be.

They explored every nook and cranny of the lighthouse, taking photos and stealing kisses. At the highest point, with the panoramic view of Seabreeze Bay spread before them, Ethan turned to Sarah, a twinkle in his eye.

"Sarah," he began, his voice filled with emotion, "I want to make this moment even more special."

Curious and filled with anticipation, Sarah watched as Ethan reached into his backpack and pulled out a small velvet box. Her heart skipped a beat as he opened it to reveal a stunning engagement ring.

"Sarah," he continued, his voice trembling with love, "I can't imagine my life without you. Will you marry me?"

Tears welled up in Sarah's eyes as she nodded vigorously. "Yes, Ethan, a thousand times yes!"

They sealed their engagement with a passionate kiss, their love shining brighter than the sun. This romantic moment marked the beginning of their new journey together, filled with hope, love, and dreams of a future intertwined.

It was a sunny Saturday morning, and Sarah and Ethan sat at the kitchen table, a sense of excitement and anticipation in the air. They had spent weeks discussing the idea of moving in together, and today, they were going to make a decision.

Ethan reached across the table and took Sarah's hand, his eyes filled with warmth. "Sarah, I've been thinking a lot about this, and I think it makes sense for us to move in together. My house has more space and is closer to town, which will be more convenient for both of us."

Sarah nodded, a smile playing on her lips. "I agree, Ethan. It's a practical decision about taking the next step in our relationship. I want to wake up next to you every morning and fall asleep in your arms every night."

Ethan's heart swelled with affection. "That's exactly how I feel, Sarah."

They spent the rest of the morning planning the logistics of the move, discussing what furniture they would keep and what they would sell or donate. They talked about how they would divide household responsibilities and what personal touches they would add to make the house feel theirs.

A few weeks later, the moving day had arrived. Sarah and Ethan stood in front of Ethan's house, excited and nervous in their expressions. The moving truck was parked on the curb, ready to transport their belongings to their new shared home.

With a deep breath, Sarah turned to Ethan. "Are you ready for this?"

Ethan smiled and took her hand. "More than ready, Sarah."

Together, they started the process of moving in. Friends and family had gathered to help, and the day was filled with laughter and camaraderie. Furniture was carried in, boxes were unpacked, and memories were made as they settled into their new life together.

As they placed their belongings side by side, they couldn't help but feel that this was a new beginning, a fresh chapter in their love story. As the sun set on their first day in their new home, Sarah and Ethan sat on the porch swing, their fingers intertwined, watching the stars emerge in the night sky.

Their journey was beginning, and they knew that with each passing day, their love would grow stronger in their shared home, surrounded by the memories they were creating together.

Sarah and Ethan decided to host a small gathering at their newly shared home to announce their engagement and share their plans for the future with their closest friends and the Seabreeze Bay community. They believed that their love story was a testament to the magic of Seabreeze Bay and wanted to celebrate it with those who had supported them along the way.

As the sun set, their friends and neighbors gathered in their backyard, where fairy lights hung from the trees, casting a warm and inviting glow. The tables were set up with delicious food and drinks, and excitement filled the air.

Sarah and Ethan stood hand in hand in front of their loved ones. Sarah's engagement ring glistened in the soft evening light. She cleared her throat, her heart filled with joy. "Thank you all for being here tonight. As most of you know, Ethan and I have been on quite a journey, and it's brought us closer together in ways we never imagined."

Ethan chimed in, his voice filled with love and gratitude. "Seabreeze Bay has been the backdrop of our love story, and we wanted to share some exciting news with all of you." He turned to Sarah, a twinkle in his eye, and dropped to one knee. "Sarah, will you marry me?"

Tears of joy welled up in Sarah's eyes as she nodded vigorously. "Yes, Ethan, a thousand times yes!"

Their friends and neighbors erupted in cheers and applause. Hugs and congratulations were exchanged as the couple shared their happiness with those who had become like family in Seabreeze Bay.

Amid the celebration, Sarah and Ethan shared their plans for a world-traveling honeymoon and the adventures they hoped to embark on together. Their loved ones were thrilled for them, offering their support and well-wishes for this new chapter in their lives.

As the night continued, under the starry Seabreeze Bay sky, Sarah and Ethan danced together, their hearts brimming with love and gratitude for the community that had brought them together and the love that would carry them forward into their happily ever after.

As the candlelight flickered and the aroma of their favorite dishes filled the air, Sarah and Ethan sat across from each other at their cherished seaside restaurant. The atmosphere was tinged with romance, and their hearts were filled with dreams of their future together.

Ethan reached across the table, his fingers gently grazing Sarah's hand. "Can you believe it, Sarah? We're engaged, and our future is wide open."

Sarah smiled, her eyes sparkling with excitement. "I know, Ethan, it's almost surreal. We've come so far, and I couldn't be happier." She sipped her wine, her mind already wandering to their next adventure. "Where do you want to go on our around-the-world honeymoon?"

Ethan's face lit up as he began to share his dreams. "Well, first, I was thinking we could start in Europe. Paris, the City of Love, of course. We'll stroll along the Seine, visit the Eiffel Tower, and indulge in croissants at a cozy café."

Sarah's eyes sparkled with excitement as she added, "And then we can head to Italy. Explore the romantic canals of Venice, savor authentic pizza in Naples, and admire the art in Florence."

Ethan nodded eagerly. "Exactly! And after that, we could venture into the exotic landscapes of Southeast Asia.

Picture us exploring the ancient temples in Cambodia, sailing through the stunning Halong Bay in Vietnam, and getting lost in the vibrant streets of Bangkok."

Sarah's imagination ran wild as she continued, "And let's not forget about the breathtaking natural wonders. We can hike the Inca Trail to Machu Picchu, go on a safari in Africa, and relax on the pristine beaches of the Maldives."

Their dreams became more vivid with each passing moment, and the warmth of their shared vision illuminated their faces. Their honeymoon wasn't just a trip; it was a journey they would embark on together, exploring the wonders of the world hand in hand.

Ethan reached across the table again, his eyes locked onto Sarah's. "And through all these adventures, we'll make memories that will last a lifetime."

Sarah's heart swelled with love as she whispered, "I can't wait to see the world with you, Ethan, and build a life filled with love, adventure, and unforgettable moments."

Their dreams of an around-the-world honeymoon were not just fantasies but plans in motion. Their love and anticipation for the adventures ahead deepened as they continued discussing their travel itinerary and budgeting strategies. Together, they were ready to embark on this incredible journey and create a lifetime of cherished memories.

Months passed, and Sarah and Ethan continued to plan their dream honeymoon while settling into their new life together. They had moved into Ethan's cozy house by the bay, where their love and laughter filled every room.

One crisp morning, they stood on the deck, looking at the tranquil Seabreeze Bay. The sun cast a warm, golden glow on the water, and the gentle waves whispered secrets of the sea.

Ethan wrapped his arms around Sarah, pulling her close. "Can you believe this is our home now?" he murmured, his voice filled with contentment.

Sarah leaned into his embrace, her heart full of gratitude. "It's perfect, Ethan. Our little piece of paradise."

They knew their journey was far from over as they stood there, wrapped in each other's love. The adventures they had planned, the challenges they would face, and the love they shared would continue to shape their story.

With a sense of endless possibilities and the promise of a love that could weather any storm, Sarah and Ethan knew that their happily ever after was beginning. And as they watched the sun rise over Seabreeze Bay, they held onto each other, ready to face whatever the future had in store.

The End

ABOUT CRYSTAL SKY

For years, Crystal has delved into the secrets of the night sky, studying and researching the stars. Her expertise as an astrologer earned her a global following, as she shared her celestial insights with enthusiasts worldwide. While her professional life centers on writing 12 yearly daily horoscope books for each star sign, "Whispers of Midnight" marks Crystal's debut into fiction—a heartfelt and captivating tale that blends her passion for astrology with an enchanting romance.

Crystal's second short book, "Starlit Whispers," is a tale of love transcending space and time, reminding us that the stars may conspire to unite two hearts. Crystal Sky invites you to explore the mysteries of the cosmos and the boundless possibilities of the human heart in this enchanting romance.

"Whispers of Seabreeze Bay" is Crystal's debut full-length romantic fiction novel.

Whispers of Seabreeze Bay